The Missing Sea Captain

A Yolanda's Yummery Cozy Mystery

Book Two

Lisa Maliga

Book Description

The successful launch of Yolanda's Yummery in the trendy Brentwood area of Los Angeles has Yolanda Carter working seven days a week. Her delicious desserts are garnering many repeat customers and in just a few weeks the adjoining Beverage Bar will be opening. She's involved in a budding romance with sophisticated British tea baron, Nigel Garvey.

The mystery involves Captain Angus, a regular homeless customer who disappears. Clues point toward Yolanda being involved in foul play. Lead investigator Detective Churchill thinks she's a murderer, along with her best friend, Teagan Mishkin.

Will Yolanda's name be cleared, and can those bestselling Magical Cakes of Love save her and the yummery?

Includes two new recipes!

OTHER WORKS OF FICTION

Diary of a Hollywood Nobody
Hollywood After Dark: 3 Tales of Terror
I Almost Married a Narcissist
I WANT YOU: Seduction Emails from a Narcissist
Love Me, Need Me: A Narcissist's Tale
The Narcissist Chronicles: The WHOLE Story
North of Sunset
Notes from Nadir
Out of the Blue
Satan's Casting Call
September Harvest
South of Sunset
Sweet Dreams

Cookbooks

PREFACE

Formerly known as *Magical Cakes of Love*, this second book in the series is a genuine cozy mystery. While the Magical Cakes of Love are still a featured item at Yolanda's Yummery, the magical secret ingredient that was touted in all the books is no longer part of the plot. There is no paranormal angle, although this series still fits into the genre of a sweet romance/cozy mystery.

Since beginning this series back in 2014, I've learned a lot more about baking. I was able to test out various recipes and a couple of years later I became so obsessed with macarons that I ended up writing not one but two cookbooks about these lovely French pastries. However, in the former edition of this book, the only recipe I managed to give out was a lemon coconut oats energy bar recipe. I've since scrapped that and have gone with a recipe for chocolate energy bars and Valencia orange cupcakes with buttercream frosting.

CHAPTER 1

TUESDAY, EARLY JUNE

"I still can't tell whether it's the middle of the night or the middle of the morning," said Yolanda Carter, the owner of Yolanda's Yummery. She was addressing BB Gustafson, the plump young assistant pastry chef who had just been let inside the bakery's front door. Beneath the cupcake shaped clock that read 3:01, the younger employee was smiling, and the froth of curly ash blonde hair was tied back with a pink ribbon that matched her T-shirt. Her heart-shaped face was aglow with the warmth of her upbeat personality as she giggled at Yolanda's statement.

"You're right, I can't tell either!" In the parking lot behind her were a few cars and trucks beneath one of the tall light poles. Mist glistened on the vehicles surfaces and kept the asphalt shiny in the three-hour-old Tuesday morning. Inside the bright and warm yummery, the mixing of the ingredients would commence, and the Magical Cakes of Love would be baked along with dozens of cookies, brownies, and cupcakes.

All wasn't quiet in the yummery as next door the empty storefront was three weeks away from being turned into the Beverage Bar. The nonalcoholic assortment of drinks would

1

range from imported coffees and teas to smoothies, malts, shakes and ice cream sodas. From ten at night to six in the morning, the once quiet store to the west was now a-clatter with whining buzz saws, lots of hammering and pounding, and assorted construction noises. The man in charge was Gil Resnick, general building contractor, and his team of two younger carpenters: Lance Norton and Pepe Menendez.

Gil strode into the yummery through the open area the size of a large double door and called out, "Morning, ladies! Nice of you sweeties to join us!"

"Morning, Gil. Coffee will be ready in a minute." Yolanda hid her grimace at the loud noises and voice she encountered the instant she arrived every morning after her twenty-five-minute drive from her home in Sherman Oaks. She was of average height and had extra weight on her hips that wouldn't go away, even when she was working in the kitchen over twelve hours a day. The young woman had warm hazel eyes and long chestnut brown hair pulled back into a ponytail.

BB's smile was unwavering as she greeted the boisterous chief of construction. "Hey, Gil," was her meager contribution to the conversation as she was shy around men, especially such a tall, rangy man with leering indigo eyes. A man old enough to be her father and wearing a wedding band. *Off limits*, BB's mama would have said.

BB went into the small employee's lounge at the back of the kitchen. Eight lockers lined part of a wall, and a perky yellow table and four matching chairs were on the opposite side. Colorful pegs stuck in the wall sported the employees' aprons and jackets. BB always found the room quiet as it was the furthest spot away from the hubbub of a busy bakery, or as it was always referred to as the yummery due to all the sugary goodies found within the new Brentwood store.

BB looked at the large two-burner commercial coffee

maker and the glass decanter was dark with the rich Fair Trade roast Costa Rican coffee guaranteed to wake up any sleepy employee or customer. Oops, she had better not even think the word customer as Yolanda called anyone who walked through the front door an appreciated guest. BB liked that term the instant she heard it, which happened to be last Monday. She was interviewed on Monday, began work on Tuesday, and today began her second week on the job. It was a whirlwind for the teenager who had only arrived in Los Angeles in mid-May. The big city was a two-day drive from Clarktown, Oklahoma.

After putting her purse and knapsack in a locker, she pulled out her notebook and pen, tied on her pink apron, and went into the back of the store where the current beverage area was wedged between the curved glass cases that showed off the colorful array of baked goods. Everyone had his or her own coffee mug with the logo. It was part of the welcome package each employee received. She had been delighted to open the pink canvas tote bag and find the mug along with two T-shirts, an apron and some lotion and soap made by Heather Hathaway's Lotions & More. Heather Hathaway was a friend of Yolanda's who also got her start in the kitchen making lotions from scratch.

BB took charge and poured everyone's coffee. Chubby Pepe with the incredibly thick jet-black hair and a goatee, shyly approached her; she felt her face flush, her arm shook, and she concentrated on keeping the pot steady. He sniffed the steaming hot contents and gave her a big toothsome grin. "Thank you amiga," he said. "You make very good coffee."

"Thank you but I just added it to the machine," she patted the surface. "It does all the work." She smiled; her dimpled chin and cheeks making her look even younger than her eighteen years.

"Speaking of which," said Yolanda as she added a sugar cube to her morning coffee. "Let's get bakin'!"

She and BB gave each other a high five. "You learn fast, sister," said Yolanda. "Just like Rita."

BB smiled and nodded. "Thanks. From what you told me, Rita sounded really neat."

"She was – and a natural baker like us. She learned to bake when she was a kid. She never went to culinary school. Too bad her husband was transferred to Germany. But that's life in the army--never know where you'll be stationed."

Yolanda sighed, remembering how much fun it was to work with Rita, who was in her mid-thirties and had a daughter in high school. Rita had a maturity that allowed her to effortlessly give and take orders. Even in the three months she worked there, she had relied on the woman's common sense in helping run the yummery from dealing with appreciated guests to the vendors and staff members.

While BB was brilliant in the kitchen, she was so naïve about people that she almost gave Captain Angus her last dollar when he showed up, reeking of cheap booze mixed with tobacco and Eau de Body Odor. The thought of slipping him some cupcake shaped soap, the only kind Yolanda carried in the Gift Corner, was tempting but she didn't want to alienate him. After all, he was a paying appreciated guest. Even if he picked coins out of fountains and off the street and panhandled the paper money. Although impoverished, he had feelings. Old Captain Angus was "bad off," as Teagan Mishkin, her longtime friend and the yummery's perky part time counter girl, had once commented. The captain had a crush on Teagan, who worked a few evenings and weekends as an exotic dancer at the Wicked Fun Gentlemen's Club. Teagan was extremely interested in being seen and went out to auditions for acting and modeling parts. Her biggest goal was to marry or live with a rich man, but she was currently between multi-millionaires.

The hammering and banging noises began as soon as the three men returned to the future Beverage Bar, but the commercial Hobart mixers that mixed and whipped the day's sweets and treats would drown out the annoying construction sounds. Yolanda opened her recipe box that she kept locked in her office and pulled out an old-fashioned lined index card with the penciled in recipe for the new energy bars. It was the second day of the energy bar debut and yesterday's batch of the gluten-free energy-based bars had sold out before noon. There were only two varieties, plain and chocolate chip, but she'd debuted with the right flavors.

They diligently baked until six o'clock, making the batters for the Magical Cakes of Love including the featured flavor of the week: Valencia orange. The crate of Valencia oranges in the corner of the kitchen was reserved exclusively for the Valencia orange cupcakes, cookies, and Magical Cakes of Love. The juicer was being worked hard, and BB was getting very adept at zesting the peels for the topping.

"Nothing like a citrusy way to start the day!" said Yolanda, gazing at the baked goods that would soon fill the cases. She glanced at the clock on the wall. "It's already six o'clock! Break time!" Yolanda was a workaholic, but she knew when it was time to sit down and rest or go outside and breathe in the fresh morning air after a night of light rain.

BB was putting all the trays showing off the bright orange bakery goods topped with the orange zest, into the walk-in refrigerator. There they would sit for about thirty minutes, cooling off before being placed in their final resting space: behind the super clean glass display cases where they'd be admired and then sold. The kitchen was filled with the aroma of sweet Valencia oranges and three noses from next door sniffed mightily as BB garnished the last cupcake with a sprinkle of fresh orange shavings. Gil was the first to knock on the side of the double door in progress, a mere formality, and walk into the kitchen to see the abundance of the day's goodies.

"Lookin' good! Can I buy an orange cupcake?" Gil asked.

"Not for sale now! And I think maybe Lance and Pepe might like one too?" Yolanda was approaching the tray that was on the stainless steel table near the walk-in refrigerator. Gil pulled out his wallet and Yolanda smiled and shook her head. "Free first cupcakes of the day policy." She paused as Gil picked up two cupcakes and passed them to his employees and grabbed a third for himself.

"Go on, BB, you made these." Yolanda grinned and watched as around her the cupcakes were consumed in a matter of seconds. Lance had an orange mustache until he licked it away after Pepe pointed it out. BB chuckled. "Thanks, Yolanda." She took one off the tray and had a small bite.

"Next time we do this flavor we should make these filled with an orange vanilla frosting..." Yolanda looked at the cupcakes, picked up the tray, and headed towards the fridge. "Yeah, this is giving me an idea..."

"Uh oh," BB joked when she saw her boss walking into the cooler like a sleepwalker.

"Well, time to pack up and call it a night," said Lance, looking at BB with a wide grin, removing his white hardhat to reveal coppery hair tied back in a ponytail. "How late are you working, BB?"

BB glanced at the older man's snug and faded jeans clinging to his muscular legs and the blue tank top showing off his strong chest and arms. Oh, he looked so good... "I'm here 'til noon or so," she didn't want to appear too interested in the good-looking dude.

Yolanda snapped out of her recipe-induced trance when she briskly stepped out of the fridge and closed the door behind her. "I think maybe eleven thirty because Teagan will be in then." She noted how he was preening for BB.

"I think it's supposed to be about seventy degrees and partly sunny—a good day to go to the beach…"

BB looked awkwardly at Lance. "Yeah, sounds great."

"Awesome, gotta go down to Hermosa and catch the waves. Later, dudes!" He threw the liner into the trashcan. Lance went into the half-finished store to pick up his lunch tote and tool belt, hanging it over one shoulder as he turned and waved, heading for the back door. "See ya later!" The door closed behind him and a minute later BB noticed his red Toyota RAV4 screeching out of the parking lot onto San Vicente Boulevard and sighed as it disappeared from her line of vision.

"I guess he doesn't want to go out with me."

"He's just put in a full night's work, BB. He probably wants to surf, have breakfast, and get some sleep," Yolanda said. "But it could be in any order!"

BB was slumping as she and Yolanda headed for the break room. "That's true. He's night shift, I'm day shift. Maybe his next job will be day shift and we can go out then." She went to her locker and opened it.

"Maybe," Yolanda said as she went over to the table and sat down.

"He sure is cute. And I kinda wanted to go to the beach with him. I never saw the ocean until I got here last month."

Yolanda stared at her for a couple of seconds. "It seems so strange, but I guess being in the middle of Oklahoma makes sense. I grew up seeing the ocean all the time in Laguna Beach."

Yolanda's parents lived in Laguna Beach where Frederick Carter was a glassblower who created hand blown creations. His cake stands were sold in the yummery and in his private studio. He also made cookie jars, glasses, and jewelry. Formerly a top-selling realtor, he now supported himself and her mother with his artistry. Her mother taught Pilates and owned Abby's Batik Creations, another artistic endeavor where she created unique silk and cotton fabric designs.

Last year, Yolanda was up against Freeze N Bake, an established company that dealt with "fresh, frozen products" that were sold in supermarkets and later heated up in the oven by the consumer. Their ingredients were heavy on preservatives and cheap fillers and when they sponsored the Great Brownie Taste-off, Yolanda's brownies competed against theirs. Due to her high quality, fresh ingredients, and baking skill, she won.

During their early morning break, BB returned her notebook and pen to her locker, having written down more recipes and instructions, and read a chapter of a romance novel. Yolanda went for a walk around the perimeter of the Brentwood Grove Shoppes mini mall. She was always trying to whittle away those extra pounds that stubbornly clung to her hips. Walking around that early June morning and seeing the blossoming purple jacaranda flowers on the trees made her realize how fortunate she was to live there. She couldn't imagine living so far inland like the small town in Oklahoma where BB was born and raised.

Just before the store opened at seven o'clock, she admired the sparkling clean curved glass cases that showed the colorful creations. The Magical Cakes of Love were the first products the customer saw--smaller than normal nine or ten-inch round cakes that most bakeries carried. Yolanda baked the signature cakes in six-inch round pans, enough for one or two people. As the special was Valencia orange, there were dozens of those lovely orange cakes along with decadent chocolate, fancy vanilla buttercream, red velvet, and summer strawberry. In the next display case was the choice of brownies, which ranged from the prizewinning plain to those filled with chopped California walnuts or topped with a rich German chocolate frosting, the peanut butter brownie, or the new chocolate fudge mint brownie.

As soon as an appreciated guest entered Yolanda's Yummery, the Gift Corner was to their left. A spiral clothes rack featured colorful aprons, T-shirts, and tank tops bearing the cute logo. Shelves behind the clothes rack boasted a half dozen colored and transparent glass pedestal cake and cupcake stands with domed lids.

On the middle glass shelf sat four rows of bottles, advertising Heather Hathaway's Lotions & More ~ The Yolanda's Yummery Collection. Each fragrance had a small tester size available. There were also some realistic looking cupcake-shaped soaps in bakery aromas and pastel colors.

Along the right-hand wall were eight round white metal tables, each with four matching chairs around them. They lined the wall from back to front on the other side of the cookies and cupcakes display case. The striped cushions matched the pastel pink, lemon yellow, and sea foam green wallpaper.

In the grayish light of the morning, Yolanda noticed the arrival of the cars and the people who got out of them and headed for the yummery. Outside the front door stood Jeannie Stanton, a tall brown and silver haired woman wearing a yellow headband that matched her shirt. She clutched a pink Yolanda's Yummery tote bag. Yolanda smiled and unlocked the door, letting the older woman in. "Good morning, Jeannie," she said warmly.

Jeannie stepped inside and inhaled deeply. "Good morning, Yolanda, it smells heavenly in here." She looked up and saw BB walking in holding a tray of cupcakes. "Good morning, BB!"

BB greeted the woman with a big smile "Hey, Jeannie! Great to see you!"

"So glad to be here. Let me just put my bag away and I'll help you stock up the goodies and get the coffee and tea ready!" She hurried into the kitchen behind the striped curtain that BB had just shut to show that the business was about to open. It was a thin privacy barrier between the staff and the appreciated guests.

After the coffee pots were filled and the hot water dispenser heated up, the yummery was open for business. Jeannie unlocked the door and handed Yolanda her keys and all three employees were happy to let in almost a dozen appreciated guests.

Al and Hilda Goldberg led the way, the senior citizens sporting matching black and white designer tracksuits and spotless cross trainers. He was the same petite size as his wife and his baseball cap hid his hairless head. Hilda had abundant champagne blonde curls that framed her well made-up face. Al went over to the counter in front of the cash register located between the two main display cases. In his hand was his platinum bankcard, which he passed to his wife. "Morning, ladies. Two cupcakes, please. One chocolate. And the healthier vanilla one."

"Now, dear, you know that dark chocolate is quite healthy as it's filled with antioxidants. I saw it on PBS, so it must be true," said Hilda.

"And sugar," he said, looking at Yolanda. "Right, Yolanda?"

Yolanda smiled as she removed the first two cupcakes of the day with a wax paper tissue and carefully added them to a small, handled box that sported the yummery's logo. "Both types of cupcakes contain some organic sugar. We use seventy-one percent cacao chocolate so there's not that much sugar."

Hilda elbowed her husband in the ribs. "See?" she said in

her honking New York accent. "What did I tell ya? Not that much sugar. So go on, be an old fart and say no to chocolate. Me, I'm never gonna say no to chocolate!"

Al patted his stomach, standing straighter as he did so, and unzipped his jacket. His white shirt was tucked into his warm-up pants. He pivoted so that anyone within view could see his trim midsection. Then he reached over and patted her stomach, which protruded noticeably. "Well, who here has the flat tummy?"

A woman in a tan suit paired with a black blouse stepped toward the cookie and cupcake area past the couple. Lydia Sloan's brown hair was swept back into a bun and smoky gray eye shadow emphasized her dark eyes, which contrasted with her pallid complexion. She smiled at the older couple. "I think you both look great."

"Hear that, wise guy?" Hilda said, thrusting her chest up and lifting her arms above her head. "And who can still touch her toes?" She reached forward with her arms and swiftly bent over until her fingertips touched the tops of her shoes.

There was a smattering of applause, most of it from behind the counter. Jeannie grinned. "Now that's impressive."

BB and Yolanda both chimed in with their approval. "Gosh, Mrs. Goldberg, I wish I could do that," BB said.

Hilda had slowly risen to her full four feet eleven inches; her face flushed almost the same shade as her burgundy lips. "My goodness, dearie, you're still a child, of course you can."

A young couple dressed in business attire watched the proceedings and ambled over to gaze at the Magical Cakes of Love in the front display case. Yolanda went over and consulted with them.

"Excuse me, but can I get my usual fancy vanilla buttercream cupcake and a small coffee?" Lydia asked.

Lydia's voice had an edge to it that motivated Jeannie to

wait on her even faster than usual and BB quickly went over to the coffee maker and poured the freshly brewed beverage, covering it with a plastic lid.

The Goldbergs left the yummery amidst a hearty chorus of goodbyes and well wishes for a good day. Lydia ducked out after them just as a tall woman in her early forties wearing a dark jacket over lime green slacks sashayed over to the cupcake area. She was followed by a tawny-haired preteen in a blue plaid skirt and crisp white blouse. "Hey BB!" called the uniformed girl as she went over to the cookie display. "Can I have a sample please?"

BB lifted the glass-domed lid from the rectangular glass tray that had just been filled with neatly cut cookie quarters. Clarabelle reached up and took a piece, glancing at her mother, and then ate the cookie bit. After she finished chewing, she said, "Yum! You make the best cookies in the world!" She giggled.

The mother cracked a smile as she looked at her daughter. "I assume you want a six-pack?"

She girl nodded, the glittery barrettes in her hair sparkling in the overhead light. "Yup, because I must give Jumping Hercules at least one oatmeal raisin cookie. He likes them even better than apples."

"Just make sure you don't eat all those cookies for lunch—they're for dessert."

Clarabelle rolled her eyes. "Moooom, I know that! Duh!"

"I'll also have two of your Valencia orange cupcakes, please," the mother said to BB. BB went to the back wall where the multicolored cellophane bags displayed the popular Yolanda's yummy 6-pack cookie stack. Yolanda had come up with the idea to offer some packets of cookies and they all sported a matching ribbon and a colorful hangtag. The freshly baked cookies were chosen for either the stacks or the display case. If there were any leftovers at six in the evening, they would automatically go into the cookie stacks the following day. While the varieties changed with the flavor of the week, the standards always included oatmeal raisin, double chocolate chip, and peanut butter. Today there was the addition of frosted Valencia orange sugar cookies in a neon orange bag that was guaranteed to sell out, according to Jeannie who reported that happened Monday evening.

Around ten o'clock, Yolanda went to her small office with a view of the kitchen. She left the door open and sat down behind her desk to do paperwork. She kept everything organized into IN and OUT bins and the color-coded filing system was helpful for her visually. Picking up the green 'Teas' folder, she couldn't help thinking of her boyfriend of four months, Nigel Garvey. He was the grandson or was it the great-grandson, of the founder of the venerable London-based Garvey Coffee & Tea Merchants, Ltd. Founded back in 1901, they specialized in a huge assortment of teas and coffees from all the continents of the world. Yolanda was going to be stocking a rotating assortment of their superior quality teas and coffees for the Beverage Bar. She had their extensive catalogue on file and pulled it out, noting several pages dedicated to teas from India.

Excellent selection, she thought, closing the catalogue, and putting the folder down on the pile, reaching for the brown one beneath it labeled 'Coffee & Chocolate'. A large, lavishly photographed catalogue showed closeups of coffee beans and cacao pods along with the finished products of steaming hot coffee cups and mugs and several fancy glasses filled with dark chocolate topped with whipped cream. Chocolate peppermint blizzard was a Christmas-themed red mug with a dollop of whipped cream sprinkled with green and red peppermint bits. "Yum, great idea, and even better for cupcakes!" she said quietly. Quickly flipping through it, she stopped near the back to see what types of chocolate were offered and was pleased to note that French chocolatier Valrhona was listed, and several types of drinking chocolate would be available at the Beverage Bar.

She closed the folder and reached for the next one on the pile, which happened to be lavender. Without opening it, she knew what that meant: a specialty wedding cake for her best friend Heather Hathaway's older sister. Ordinarily, Yolanda didn't make wedding cakes, but the founder of Heather's Lotions & More had only one sister and wanted to make Rosemary's wedding memorable with a purple and white four-tier cake. Yolanda had finally figured out the unique design for the concoction that had to be finished by the third Saturday in July.

Yolanda sighed as she thought about Nigel. On her desk was a small, framed photo of them with their arms around each other. It was taken when they were at Malibu Beach. The sun emphasized his natural golden highlights. She smiled, admiring his classical features, and piercing dark eyes. The man had such a bright, winsome smile. He was so sexy and so handsome, but the time they spent together was limited. He worked long hours, too. But they had the mutual goal of opening the Beverage Bar in late June. She decided that a dual celebration of the grand opening along with her birthday was an effective way to launch it. Once the addition to the yummery was complete they could see each other more. She would soon be twenty-eight years old, and her mother had been married by then. Nigel was two years younger than she was, but that was fine. On the cat-themed desk calendar she saw at the bottom of the page the red notation: 7:30 Nigel, Skate Palace. Glancing at the clock, she thought that in only a few more hours they'd see each other in person.

* * *

Nick Delany shuffled into the yummery that afternoon. He wore his yellow shirt uniform paired with baggy cargo shorts and black slip-on sneakers. "Hey Jeannie," he said, giving her a toothsome grin. He ambled to the back and went behind the counter and up to the striped curtain. "I emailed my paper in early."

"Hello, Nick. Good to see you," said Jeannie. "Back when I was in school, I had to use a manual typewriter. It took me so long to type up and I had to hand it in to my professor."

"Wow, a *manual* typewriter?" he shook his head. "I can't imagine that!"

She smiled at the young man and went back to boxing a Valencia orange Magical Cake of Love. A young woman in a floral-patterned dress picked up the pink box. "It's my boyfriend's birthday—so I think this'll make a great dessert."

Jeannie nodded. "I couldn't agree more."

As the woman left the yummery, Nick approached the counter, tying on his green apron. "She's hot," he said as the slender woman hurried out to the parking lot.

"You say that about any woman under the age of fifty," she said.

"Hey Jeannie, I think it's time to change the tips sign again. I think we should do it every day – catch people's attention that way."

Jeannie glanced up at the cupcake shaped clock above the door. "You're probably right. Anything to increase the tips is always a good idea."

He pulled out a neon yellow piece of paper and affixed it to the glass jar. "I printed this before I left home 'cause I want it to get our appreciated guests' attention."

TIPPING IS VERY GOOD FOR YOU!

Yolanda stepped out of the kitchen holding a tray full of chocolate mint brownies. She glanced at the sign that he taped on the jar. Jeannie leaned over and looked. Both women laughed. Just then, the door opened, and Lydia walked in followed by a couple of teenage girls in miniskirts that caught Nick's attention.

Lydia went to the front area where the Magical Cakes of Love were displayed. She pointed at the nearest cake. "I need one of these for my boss. It's his anniversary."

Amidst lots of giggling and sampling of cookies, the girls were soon carrying bags holding many 6-pack cookie stacks along with several other types of cookies and brownies.

The rest of the afternoon went by at a brisk pace as appreciated guests drifted in and emerged snacking on cupcakes or the cookies and the boxed Magical Cakes of Love were sold out of the popular Valencia orange flavor just before closing time. The tips jar was attracting more coins and bills. Nick was moving around filling orders as quickly as he could.

Only a few items remained, and as Yolanda would be seeing Nigel that night, she knew he'd want to try the Valencia orange so that he could determine what teas and coffees would pair up with it when it would again be offered as a flavor of the week later that summer.

She went to the door to lock it for the evening when a young strawberry blonde woman wearing black skinny jeans with turquoise ballet flats approached. She waved as she opened the door. "Hey Yolanda!" She stepped inside and they briefly hugged.

"Hey Heather! Great to see you." Yolanda smiled. "Your products are really selling well."

"That's so good to know. I'm going to be sending you some new ones to test. I'm really excited about it."

A shorter woman with dyed black hair pulled into a stubby ponytail walked in, looking around. She wore a shapeless mauve sundress paired with black sneakers. "So, this is the yummery," Rosemary said. "Kinda on the small side..." She walked over to the display case and saw only three Magical Cakes of Love and barely a dozen brownies. "Did we come at a bad time?" Rosemary asked, her forehead wrinkling.

"Rosemary! So nice to see the bride-to-be," Yolanda said to the disgruntled woman. "Well, no, you came at the end of the day. I was just going to put everything in the fridge, but I made sure to save you a decadent chocolate and a fancy vanilla buttercream Magical Cake of Love to test." She gestured, moving towards the back of the store. "Let's go back to my office and we'll sample them."

Thirty minutes later, and the three women were still in Yolanda's office with the two cakes cut into several slices.

"Now, I tried on 129 wedding dresses before I found the perfect one..." Rosemary commented, taking another bite of the chocolate cake slice on a paper plate. "It was a nightmare trying to get one in my petite size and style because I wanted the Sweetheart Serenade model. It's ecru lace with puffed sleeves edged with rhinestones and pearls and a white silk crinoline skirt with a detachable twenty-foot lace train edged with pearls...oh you'd think I was looking for something unusual!" She sighed and rolled her big watery blue-gray eyes. Rosemary pulled out her iPhone and punched the screen a few times. "Here's the winning dress..." She turned the phone's screen, so it faced Yolanda and a blurry shot of some off-white creampuff meringue of a bridal gown was seen.

"That looks nice," Yolanda stated diplomatically, glad when the phone was removed from her line of vision.

"Well, it should. Oh, and the cathedral length veil is going to be just as spectacular with it being longer than the train and studded with Swarovski crystals. And let me tell you about the sixty-one punch recipes I searched for before I finally found the right one. And I think the florist is going to be changing again real soon..." She enjoyed another bite of her cake, paused, and took another. She sighed loudly. "You'd think people could handle brides changing their minds occasionally."

Heather rolled her eyes, and delicately bit into her slice of fancy vanilla buttercream. "This is so good, Yo. I don't know how you stay so skinny."

Rosemary noted the lavender file folder and pointed at it. "The wedding cake colors will be pale plum, flaming hot orange, mist blue, and ecru, right? Oh, and five tiers, so maybe emerald green as another color?"

Yolanda opened it and looked at the notes she'd made. "No, I have a violet and cream four-tier cake."

Rosemary shook her head. "Nope, I know I said to both you and Heather five tiers. And I don't want just any pale plum; I want a light to almost medium purple like a purple gray. Then I want, hang on..." she touched the phone's screen twice and handed it to Yolanda. "Here is the color combo."

Yolanda looked and her eyes widened in surprise. The five different colors looked horrendous.

"Are you sure?" She handed the phone back to Rosemary.

"Yes, I'm sure. I showed it to Heather, and she said the same thing. It's MY wedding and this is what I want!"

"I understand, Rosemary. Do you like your cake? Maybe you'd like some more?"

"Yeah, I like my cake and I want both vanilla and chocolate in alternating layers."

"That can easily be done." Yolanda agreed, making notes on the paper with the wedding cake information.

"Good. That's what I want to hear more of! And just to clarify, this cake is free, right?"

Yolanda nodded. "Yes, I'm doing it as a favor to Heather."

Yolanda's phone rang and she eagerly answered it. "Just one minute, please!" She grabbed her cell phone and left the office, heading back to the break room. "Hey Nigel. Right, okay. In about fifteen minutes. I'm dealing with a bride-to-be."

"Good luck with that," the English-accented voice of her boyfriend trailed off into laughter and the call ended.

Nigel and Yolanda had agreed to meet at the Skate Palace at the edge of Santa Monica. She saw his new silver Lexus SUV parked near the side of the large building. He was sitting in his vehicle with the driver's side window halfway open. As she walked over to him, she noticed he wore neon green earbuds. He was immersed in listening to music. Nigel glanced in his side view mirror and grinned when he saw her. She jumped into the passenger seat and sat next to him. A minute later, and they were both enjoying pre-workout cupcakes, as Nigel referred to them.

He wolfed his down in two bites. Reaching over to his cupholder, he picked up his water bottle and drained the contents. "Thank you, sweetsie. Outstanding cupcake, as usual. I love the tanginess of the orange."

She blushed with pleasure after receiving the compliment. Coming from him it meant so much. "Thanks, Nigel, so glad you liked it."

"I'll skate even better—and so will you."

He crumpled the liner into a ball and got out of his vehicle. Outside the red brick building was a large trash container and he tossed it inside. The man was wearing a forest-green tracksuit and matching sneakers.

He opened the back door and pulled out a black wheeled suitcase. When they went inside the ice rink, she saw him wave to a man who stood behind the skate rental counter. It was so cold he wore a ski jacket and wool cap pulled down over his ears.

"Hey Jed, you work until closing?" asked Nigel.

The man nodded. "Pickup hockey game starts after public session and broomball after that—long night." He looked at Yolanda. "What size skates do you need?"

They went over to an area near the coffee shop with two long rows of gouged wooden benches. Nigel opened his suitcase and pulled out a pair of black figure skates with matching terrycloth covers over the blades. She watched him put them on and adjust the long laces, doubling the knot and shoving the ends under the top part of the laces. She'd always tied the extra length of laces around the ankles.

On the smooth slippery surface, he held her hand and the energy pulsated between them as they made their way around the rink. She was blissfully unaware of anyone else as it was just her and Nigel slowly skating counterclockwise. Pop music played. She felt him gliding closer to her as he put his jacketed arm around her. She breathed in his aroma of a woodsy spice cologne and the undertone of the cupcake he'd recently eaten. The song's tempo accelerated and so did he. Nigel unwrapped his arm and an instant later was pulling her along by one hand. She held on tightly, afraid of the speed they were going, it seemed like forty miles an hour to her, someone who had only skated a couple of times before. Her blades slid out from beneath her, Yolanda felt herself falling backwards, and a second later, she fell on her rear end and slid across the frozen surface and into the wall. A miniature wave of ice particles covered her jeans as Nigel stopped within an inch of her, then reached down and pulled her upright. They stood near the wall and hugged one another, her heart pounding from the suddenness of the fall. He was closer than before.

"I'm so sorry, Yo, I didn't mean to do that..."

The words hung in the air as the hug loosened and he pulled away. "I just want to skate to this song by myself...I'll be right back."

She smiled, leaning against the scuffed wall that had been hit countess times by other skaters, watching her boyfriend expertly stroking around the ice, each stroke of the blade propelling him faster and faster.

Just how fast is he going, she thought. It made her a bit nervous to watch him speeding around, pausing to jump into the air and land on one foot. It was amazing what he could do wearing only a pair of boots and thin blades.

She lost count of how many revolutions he turned in the air.

A woman with alabaster skin and a huge burgundy bow covering the back of her blonde hair stopped by followed by a slender dark-haired man of indeterminate age. Her slender figure was emphasized in a burgundy velvet dress with a knee-length flowing chiffon skirt. The man wore a black warmup outfit like Nigel's. The couple's posture was so rigid that Yolanda straightened her slouched shoulders.

Nigel completed another jump, his landing heavier and his arms flailing as he managed to retain his balance. He shook his head, looked down at the ice, and returned to the barrier and did a quick hockey stop, spraying his girlfriend with a wave of ice particles.

"Bloody triple axel's giving me problems again." He sighed. "And the quad toe loop's on vacation."

"You're a fantastic skater," the woman said before Yolanda had a chance to make a comment.

"You're too kind, Eleanor." He nodded at her and addressed the man. "Good to see you, Dean."

"Thank you, Nigel. We're working on our Viennese Waltz

for the gold level test so we can compete at that level at adult nationals next year," Eleanor said.

"That's my girl, always planning ahead," Dean hugged his partner and gave her a quick kiss on the cheek. "I don't know what I'd do without her."

Yolanda smiled but said nothing, as she was with new people and in an unfamiliar environment. A cold one, as she looked over at the wall and saw that the thermometer read fifty-five degrees. Not quite refrigeration level, but close. *It would be a good place to store chocolate*, she thought.

The couple chatted about technical terms like inside reverse rockers, brackets, and twizzles flew high overhead, not being grasped by the young baker. She saw the heavy foundation the woman wore and the crinkling edges around her eyes and mouth indicated she was probably her mother's age. Suddenly they all chuckled.

"Yes, absolutely!" Dean was animatedly nodding and then swept his arm dramatically to the right. "Those vending machines are almost worthless. Have you ever had a lukewarm cup of coffee from one of those?"

There was a chorus of laughter as Yolanda was able to appreciate that joke. No way would she ever drink anything from a vending machine.

"What's worse than lukewarm water from a vending machine? A bag of stale mini chocolate chip cookies."

More laughter from the ice skaters and Nigel gave her a friendly pat on the shoulder.

"Dean and Eleanor, this is Yolanda Carter, owner of Yolanda's Yummery and my business partner for the upcoming Beverage Bar!"

"Fancy that!" Dean said, giving her the once-over. "You're Yolanda Yummery! Next time I'm in Brentwood I'm going to try out some of your cupcakes and brownies. Nothing like freshly baked."

"Dean, you must watch your caloric intake. We need to be in tip top shape for the Jubilee on Ice show in September."

The man's narrow face reddened, but he kept his voice even. "I think a little splurge here and there is fine. We're not competing for the Olympics like Nigel is."

CHAPTER 2

WEDNESDAY

That afternoon the overcast day turned sunny. Teagan Mishkin walked in for her afternoon shift. She wore a snug French cut mint-green logoed T-shirt, tight yellow designer jeans and blush pink Italian sneakers. Her champagne blonde hair was pulled back into an elegant, braided chignon. After she clocked in, Teagan returned, tying on a yellow apron and readjusted the bib to make sure the male appreciated guests noticed her voluptuous figure.

Nick stared at her, as usual. "Hey Teagan, lookin' hot!"

Teagan smiled. "The temperature is eighty-three, you know."

"Oh, I know," Nick said. "And check out the tip of the day."

TIP O' THE DAY TO YOU!

"I see you added a smiley face, that'll help."

"It already has...see all the bills floating around in there?"

She shook her head, noticing only a few coins. "Well, it looks like I need to work my magic."

"Work it, baby!"

Yolanda flicked the curtain aside as she walked in from the kitchen carrying a tray of chocolate cupcakes. "I heard that, Nick."

Teagan rolled her eyes. "It's fine, Yo, he's …"

"Being disrespectful," Yolanda said as she put the cupcakes into the display case.

"Really, Yo, it doesn't bother me at all."

The conversation stopped as a nanny pushed a stroller inside and soon was followed by some businesspeople from the nearby office buildings. For two hours, the place was nonstop activity and at three o'clock, Lydia Sloan, clad in an elegant wine-red pantsuit, entered. She ordered her usual afternoon brownie, went back, and picked out a bottle of iced tea from the self-serve fridge unit. Teagan was moving brownies to another tray to clean the empty one. Yolanda was at the far end of the counter writing out a phone order. Nick looked at the clock above the door. "You know, I haven't seen Captain Angus all week. He's usually here twice a day…"

Teagan looked at her coworker. "Yeah, I haven't seen him either. He always leaves a tip."

"Right, he does, and he always gets the weekly special in the morning and a brownie in the afternoon. Never misses…"

Lydia stepped over to the counter carrying her iced tea. "Maybe his boat sank."

Yolanda stopped writing and looked up, puzzled. "His boat?"

A svelte woman wearing a gold and ivory-colored sundress and matching flats strode into the yummery. Her dark hair was enhanced with reddish highlights. Dani Kramer had a light tan complexion and enormous blue eyes. Her pouty lips were a shade of raspberry that contrasted sharply with her dazzling white teeth. "Hello everyone. I need my brownie fix…

I'll need two dozen in all varieties for this afternoon's meeting."

Teagan waited on the elegant woman and folded up a pink cardboard box to add the brownies.

Lydia nodded, swiping her credit card as Nick processed her order. "It's a nice boat, a yacht. Captain Angus lives on it."

Dani looked at Lydia. "I haven't seen Captain Angus around the marina lately."

Teagan placed the second row of brownies into the pink box. "He lives at the marina?"

Dani nodded. "Well, his yacht's there, yes. The man wears such disgusting rags but it's just camouflage. He's got the most beautiful Sunseeker yacht, and he can afford it. He's a Prescott. He's so rich and he's never had to work a day in his life."

Teagan sealed the box and looked at Dani. Lydia also stared at the elegantly dressed woman as she picked up her little bag and held her cold glass tea bottle. "Angus Prescott comes from the movie family," Lydia said.

"I'd also like four of your yummy cookie stacks, any type will do," Dani said. Just then, Yolanda approached to help pick out four different colored stacks, making sure the last orange one went to the appreciated guest.

"You mean Prescott Moving Pictures?" asked Teagan. "They did all those movies way back in the day?"

"Great Scott! It's a Prescott...moving picture," said Dani with a laugh. "Oh yeah, old Angus is the grandson of George Prescott, the founder. Angus is a total trust fund baby. From what I understand it's a very sizable amount of money."

Lydia had quietly departed and almost walked into a gangly man on the way into the yummery. He murmured an apology. He had a thin long nose and shoulder length hair the color of caramel. The slightly darker goatee was sparse. Faded and holy kneed jeans paired with a baggy black T-shirt was his preferred fashion. Yolanda brightened when she saw him. "Hello Patrick," she said.

"Hey Yolanda, smells great in here—as usual." He was the Other Patrick Stewart, the blogger who had promoted her after exposing her competitor's shenanigans behind the Great Brownie Taste-off.

Teagan placed Dani's purchases into a pink paper tote bag, which she set on the glass countertop near the brownie samples. Yolanda stepped around the counter and was standing near Patrick and Dani. "You know, I really thought he was homeless. Especially with those old clothes...he kinda smells."

Patrick lowered his grin a notch. "I'll have you know I took a shower this morning." He went over to the counter to help himself to a cookie sample.

"No, not you, Patrick. I just found out that Captain Angus isn't homeless."

Dani pulled out her designer billfold and removed a credit card. "Oh, and I'll have a Valencia orange Magical Cake of Love, also."

Teagan pulled one on the bottom shelf out, transferring it into a box. "I remember at the grand opening he invited me back to the marina to see his yacht. I thought he was joking. Maybe he had a rowboat or a canoe. I've always thought the captain was just crazy."

"No, not at all unless it's crazy like a fox. Cheap, too. Goes to swap meets and he's a professional dumpster diver."

"We know about his dumpster diving," Yolanda said as she gestured to her left. "Caught him back there a few times."

Teagan put the cake box next to the tote bag. "He's really nice to me. I like my men rich, but they should look like it...and smell like it. But for the right amount of money, I guess I can lower my standards." She handed back Dani's credit card. "Do you need some help getting that into your car, Ms. Kramer?"

Dani nodded. "Mrs. Kramer. Please, just call me Dani. That'd be really nice, Teagan."

Teagan walked around the counter, picked up the cake box and bag, and followed Dani out the door.

"I'm clocking out now, Yolanda," Nick said.

"Okay, Nick. Thanks so much. Great job as usual."

He walked back behind the curtain and Yolanda and Patrick stood in front of the cookie display case as he sampled a few different cookie pieces. "Wow, I thought you knew that dude was an eccentric old man. Angus is old Hollywood royalty. His grandfather's movies won best picture and some best actor awards back around World War 2. The Prescott estate in Beverly Hills is vacant and falling apart. Some say it's haunted…"

Teagan returned to the store and smiled. She put a ten-dollar bill into the tips jar. "Not as much as the club, but it all helps!"

"I need to stop by the club soon," Patrick said and popped another sample into his mouth, giving her the long, lingering, once, twice, three times over.

Teagan giggled and reached down and grabbed a Valencia orange sugar cookie. "Here, Patrick, it's on the house. You gotta be twenty-one to even enter the Wicked Fun Gentlemen's Club."

He accepted the proffered cookie.

"My fair lady, I have been twenty-one for the past three years—especially on my birthday because I love getting free drinks. And, of course, cookies."

Patrick bit into the cookie and smiled, closing his eyes. He chewed it and then popped the rest of it into his mouth, savoring the sensation of the sweet and lively orange flavor and the resulting euphoric feeling. "My dear, these are the best cookies evah! I mean it. Let me buy a dozen of them please."

After he left, Yolanda watched him heading out to his car

parked at the side of the building and noticed it was a white Toyota Prius. "I thought only old people drove those cars," Yolanda commented.

Teagan shrugged. "Not my kinda car. Of course, I'd love to have an Aston Martin because not everyone drives one of those."

Yolanda shrugged. "I wonder where Patrick lives. I mean, I met him about a mile from here. And you know what's weird about Nigel is that I've never been to his house. It was kinda like that with Zac, too. I guess guys love my place better than theirs."

"Yo, that's not a great sign, you know. Wait, don't tell me, let me guess. Nigel's too busy, right?"

Yolanda nodded and sighed. "You guessed right." She looked up at the clock. "Well, I'm closing tonight. Need to make sure my cats have enough food and I'll pick up something from the store on the way home. You work tonight at the club?"

"Not tonight. I gotta get up early tomorrow for a shampoo commercial audition. In fact, I must wash my hair tonight, so it'll look just right tomorrow."

"That's great, Teagan. I hope you get the part."

Yolanda managed to leave the yummery just after six, opting to put the money in the safe instead of dropping it off at the bank. She vowed to do it as soon as it opened on Thursday morning. Her hour-long drive included a stop at the supermarket to pick up a large container of rotisserie chicken, which she'd share with her two cats Mr. Whisker and Miss Chef. Miss Chef was a classic tuxedo with the white stripe down her face and a lovely curved white smile. Her paws resembled four clean white boots and the white stripe along the front of her body was groomed several times a day. Mr. Whisker was a muscular short-haired black cat with a single white whisker amidst his black whiskers. He was a little younger than Miss Chef was and in his fourteen months of living with Yolanda, it took him a year before he was comfortable going outside in the backyard.

After leaving the supermarket with two bags of groceries, she heard her cell phone remind her for about the tenth time that she had some messages to read. She would answer then after supper. *At least it's still daylight*, Yolanda thought as she drove up to her grandparents' former cottage on the corner of Dove Drive and Willowbrook Street. She adored the pastel yellow with white gingerbread trim home with the white picket fence. Her grandparents, Lukas and Ingrid Carter, bought it back in 1952. Grandmother Ingrid left her the two-bedroom two-bathroom bungalow when she died five years ago.

She parked her new white Honda Accord in the garage. She got out, lugging the grocery bags. The back door led to her kitchen, which had new retro sky-blue appliances. A small kitchen island topped with white quartz held her precious sky-blue KitchenAid stand mixer. Two of the wooden sides of the island contained much of her baking ware and the other two had shelves containing her extensive cookbook collection. Above the back door was a chalet-style cuckoo clock. And tonight, she'd be making her final recipe for the gluten-free energy bars that would officially debut on Saturday. When she finally got around to making them her mother adored them because she had no adverse reactions. "Dear, this energy bar is marvelous," Abby said, almost inhaling it. "I mean, it just seems to taste better."

By using organic coconut sugar, the sweetness was there, and it was more mineral rich than the organic cane sugar she used in the cupcakes. The two recipes she'd make that night would be ready for her to take the samples into work the next morning. What really made it work was the high-quality

European chocolate. The Sweet Spot was the best place to buy it as the owner, Wanda Clark, offered her a bulk discount.

After she flicked on the kitchen light, she noticed two things amiss: full water and food bowls and no cats. She paused, looking around her. *I feel like I'm being watched*, she thought.

She closed the door behind her, making sure it was locked, set the bags on the counter, and called out "Miss Chef! Mr. Whisker!" She paused, kicked off her shoes, and went into the living room. On the sage green couch were two green pillows: one that matched and another in a contrasting cobalt blue. They always were propped against one of the arms but had fallen to the floor. That was odd. She saw a flash of something black. A tail, that suddenly disappeared. She bent over, looked beneath the couch, and saw the cats. "Hey guys, I'm here. I've got a special treat for you."

There was no reaction. "Chicken, fresh hot chicken. No hormones. Just succulent goodness that you carnivores are supposed to love..."

Four wide green eyes stared at her. A hiss and growl. She stood up and looked around. Behind her in the dining room stood the tall breakfront china cabinet that displayed some Wedgwood plates and Easter egg ornaments along with her father's more colorful plates and glasses, all highlighted by soft lighting and a mirrored back. Three drawers below the shelving and on each side were two small doors. One of those doors was half-open. She bent down and swung it open the rest of the way. Inside was her grandparent's small wine collection. The last time she'd even had a bottle was when Nigel visited last month, and she found a bottle of white wine from the 1980s that he thought was pretty good. Other than occasionally using it for meat or fish, Yolanda had only consumed booze once – on her twenty-first birthday. That was the night she was given free drinks in a variety of bars and bistros. Too bad her birthday had fallen on a Friday night because her Saturday was spent recovering from her first and last hangover.

No bottles of wine were missing. She shut the door, wondering why the cats would open it, but they had opened one of her lower kitchen cabinets. She peered beneath the couch again and they stared at her although they didn't growl or hiss.

Changing into her comfortable clothes, she put her pants and T-shirt into the tall wicker laundry hamper and went into the kitchen to plate the chicken and have a large strawberry smoothie. Yolanda enjoyed being able to eat and drink what she wanted instead of making dinner for someone, other than her cats, every night. Realizing that Nigel was coming over tomorrow night she knew she'd have to dress nicer and have a meal ready for him – or something to takeout. The thought of seeing Nigel made her feel the sweet anticipation. Now if only he would decide to ask her to marry him, then their relationship would grow even stronger.

THURSDAY

Yolanda printed out a yellow flyer headlined **NEW at Yolanda's Yummery ~ Gluten-Free Energy Bars!**

Al and Hilda Goldberg were the pioneers in sampling the energy bars. The older couple wore designer tracksuits—he in black, she in amethyst, along with their spotless white cross trainers. They noticed the free samples at once.

"We won't be selling these until Saturday," Yolanda said. "Right now, we're only giving out samples of the new gluten-free energy bars."

The couple grabbed a small square of the nutritious bars covered with rolled oats and sporting a thick layer of strawberry filling.

"Another yummy treat!" said Hilda. "Will this help me lose weight?"

"Maybe walking more than running your mouth will," Al griped, reaching for a second free sample. He quickly chewed it and shook his head. "Darned if these aren't the best energy bars I've eaten. What's in 'em?"

"Dearie, I don't think Yolanda's giving away her recipe."

Yolanda smiled and handed them a flyer. "No, but I list the

ingredients and there's more information about the organic coconut sugar so that you can tell all your friends about it too. I don't say it's sugar-free because it's not. But my mom can eat these without any trouble. Some people may enjoy the fact that they contain no nuts and are considered raw as they're not baked. If I didn't thoroughly taste test these myself, I wouldn't sell them here. Remember this isn't a yukkery, it's a yummery."

There was laughter at that last statement. She looked up to see the arrival of Nigel who gave her a quick hug. "You're right, it's definitely not a yukkery! Especially with the arrival of the Beverage Bar later this month."

She grinned at him and noticed his green and white striped rugby jersey and the tan chinos. "You're dressing casually today."

"I know. It's just that kind of day, so warm and sunny. I know there are casual Fridays in America, but why not casual Thursdays?"

They went into Yolanda's office and as they discussed different types of coffee grown in Costa Rica and El Salvador, she found herself wondering about spending a honeymoon in a tropical beach resort in Costa Rica, El Salvador or anywhere near the ocean...with Nigel.

After the discussion of fair-trade coffee, he presented her with some forms and brochures. "Oh, I hate to tell you this but..." his smoldering dark eyes stared at her, and then glanced down at the floor, "but I'm not going to be able to make our date tonight after all. Something's come up at the office with the shipment from Sri Lanka and I'll probably need to go to the airport to get it all sorted out..."

No romantic honeymoon in my future, she thought. Well, it wasn't a surprise, after all, they both had careers and finding time to date was difficult. She smiled and nodded. What could she say?

The energy bar samples were being rationed as per Yolanda's orders. While BB loved them, Jeannie thought they were nice but wanted to try it in peach, orange or lemon coconut, as she preferred those flavors to strawberry. Yolanda decided to make a few batches to keep up with the demand, and she'd also oblige Jeannie and make an orange-flavored energy bar.

Around noon, a few well-dressed businesspeople wandered in, tasting the samples and admiring the baked goods. At a table near the back, a teenage couple sat, the girl eating a decadent chocolate cupcake and the guy with the glasses devoured two fancy vanilla buttercream cupcakes. His laptop was open, but he gazed at the pretty brunette across the round vintage ice cream parlor table. Their hands were entwined, and the young pair emanated that first bloom of love. Yolanda envied them. It made her doubt the feelings she had for Nigel; sometimes they were so strong, other times they weren't. Even today, before he cancelled their date, she wasn't that upset about it. Was she getting jaded? Did she really love Nigel? On the other hand, did he love her less than she loved him? She looked up from filling the sample tray with the granola bars. In walked a Hispanic man of medium height with short wavy side parted hair. His intense observation of the yummery showed he was a first timer. He looked around him, from the in-love couple at the back table to the beverage case and noted the four other appreciated guests, to the counter help of Jeannie and herself. The man ambled over to the counter displaying the cookies and cupcakes and she wondered who this new appreciated guest was? Why was this man in a non-designer grey suit so inquisitive without saying a single word?

Until their eyes met. His light greenish-grey eyes gazed into hers. Thick, straight eyebrows and a serious gaze gave him an authoritative air. "I'm Detective W. E. Churchill and I'd like to speak to the owner of this establishment, miss," he said.

She smiled at him, wondering how old he was. His white shirt was immaculate and contrasted with the somber navy-blue necktie. "You're looking at her."

He paused, his eyes flitting in the direction of Jeannie who was sliding a decadent chocolate Magical Cake of Love into a box. The front door opened, and Teagan rushed in, long hair loose and flowing, cheeks reddened with extra blusher. Instead of wearing her usual tight-fitting jeans and bakery issue T-shirt, she was crammed into a bright red minidress. "Yolanda, I had a second audition this morning. I'm in the running for the part. I'm optimistic about booking it." She glanced at her iPad.

Yolanda grinned and when Teagan rushed over, they hugged. "Wonderful news, Teagan. I hope you get it."

Teagan bounced up and down and pulled away, seeing the stern looking young man staring at them. "You want a picture? It'll last longer."

Detective Churchill nodded his head. "Thank you for that information, miss. Are you the co-owner?"

"No, I just work here and audition for acting gigs until I become the next Beverly Hills housewife."

"I thought you wanted to live in Bel Air," Yolanda commented.

"True that, but I'll settle for the 90210 ZIP code."

"Are you Yolanda?" asked the detective.

Yolanda raised her hand. "Yes I am. How can I help you?"

"I have some questions about a missing person who is frequently seen coming and going from this establishment. His name is Captain Angus Prescott." He pulled a small notepad out of his suit jacket and clicked open a pen. "Is there a place where we can talk in private?" He looked around.

"Yes, back in my office. Please..." she walked to the back of the store and to the small door at the edge of the counter, opening it for him.

"Wow, I just realized I haven't seen the captain in days...did you say his last name is Prescott?"

"Yes I did, miss," he said.

Teagan tagged along. "Do you want me to change now, or do I need to talk to the detective?"

Detective Churchill turned and looked at Teagan. "Do you know Captain Angus Prescott?"

"Not really well. He stops by twice a day, but I haven't seen him in..." she looked at her iPad and consulted her calendar. "I think Monday was the last time he was here."

"Thank you Teagan, that's helpful." He jotted what she said in his notepad.

"Dude, why don't you get one of these" she pointed to her iPad. "I mean, you can key that stuff in and there are so many apps...you'll find the captain in no time."

He raised an eyebrow. "Thanks, miss, but I prefer to do things the old-fashioned way."

"Teagan, I'll talk to the detective in my office, okay?"

She saluted. "Okay, Yo. I'll do that." Teagan turned and hurried off to the break room.

Yolanda and the detective went into her office. There was enough room for him to sit comfortably in one of the two guest chairs. Again, she noticed that he was observing his surroundings. "Miss, you have a very tidy office."

She smiled. "Thank you. Yes, it's imperative to be organized. If you start off organized then it's easier to maintain." She wasn't about to close the door as she knew that what she said wasn't anything she had to hide.

"That sounds like something my mother would say." His lips curled upwards for an instant, and then he frowned as he looked down at his notepad.

"So, the Captain has been missing since Monday?"

Yolanda nodded. "Teagan's right, it's now three days. He

always is one of the first to arrive at seven and he usually shows up again at three. Sometimes I'll see him hanging out back near the dumpster.

"What else can you tell me about him?"

"Well, I thought he was homeless until yesterday. It seems like some of our appreciated guests were telling me that he lives on a boat in the marina. He's also the grandson of the founder of Prescott Moving Pictures."

"Yes, we have that information. Can you tell me anything else?"

"Sure, he liked to have brownies, he always had a sample, and then he'd buy either the plain chocolate or the peanut butter chocolate. In the afternoon he'd get either a chocolate chip cookie or a decadent chocolate cupcake."

Scribbling down what she said, he nodded. "I'm beginning to see a pattern here, miss."

"Yeah, he likes chocolate."

He smiled. "Seems like it."

"He always paid in cash, sometimes in coins. Oh, and, I don't like to say this, but well, he wasn't the cleanest person." She looked down at the calendar blotter on her desk and fidgeted with a pen, rolling it back and forth. "You know, he smelled kinda ripe."

"Like he hadn't bathed in a while?"

"Yeah, like that. And the more he moved around the more he smelled it seemed. Well, I guess I can admit it to you, but he stank. There, I've said it."

"Must have been pretty bad, huh?"

She nodded. "The captain's an appreciated guest but he'd be a lot more appreciated if he took a shower occasionally. I must be honest, I wished sometimes that he'd go somewhere else. I think sometimes he drove off other appreciated guests because of his smell. I mean, one time a woman with a super expensive designer purse and shoes just glared at him and walked out. I was so uncomfortable, and I couldn't kick him out, but..."

Churchill was hastily scribbling in his notebook. "Right. Anything else?"

Yolanda shook her head, realizing that she may have been a bit too forthright. "Not that I can think of detective." She smiled, glancing over at the tray of fresh energy bars with strawberry filling that rested on the counter before the detective arrived. She smiled at the detective and got up. "Yes, I need something from you." Picking up a knife, she scored a few rows and then cut a piece for the detective. "I'd like you to try the new energy bar. It's gluten-free."

"Miss, are you trying to bribe me?" He had followed her into the kitchen and was invariably looking around at all the equipment and she hoped he noticed how clean everything was. She had an A rating from the city and wanted to keep it. Yolanda picked up a slice with a piece of wax tissue and handed it to him. "I hope you like strawberry."

He nodded. "Yup. Total bribery. I could cite you for trying to bribe an officer of the law." He took a bite and suddenly smiled. His face glowed beneath the fluorescent lights. "Miss, this is amazing." He swallowed the rest of it and grinned. "Best energy bar I've ever had. I love the buttery flavor. It's more like a dessert than an energy bar."

"Wow, a critic!" she laughed.

"No, I'm not criticizing it. I just think it's too sweet and buttery to be an energy bar."

"Well, it's a yummery, everything here is sweet."

"Yes, miss, including you." His face reddened and he cleared his throat. "Um, what I mean is that yes, I know this bakery is a yummery and that you serve sweets...well, um, I was wondering if I could interview the other ladies that work with you?" He pointed to her office. "In there?"

"Of course." She looked at her watch. "Jeannie's due to clock out now so you should talk to her first."

Jeannie talked to the detective and gave the only information she knew. The captain preferred chocolate brownies and cupcakes most of the time and came in twice a day. She had occasionally seen him behind the store in the dumpster area.

Flirtatious Teagan didn't deviate from the facts, either. He was a regular appreciated guest who bought brownies in the morning and cupcakes or cookies in the afternoon. He also enjoyed the cookie samples. She, like all the other employees, assumed the good captain was homeless.

"Where were you on Monday night?" Churchill asked Teagan.

Teagan paused, trying to remember. "I was home."

"Right. And you live where?"

"I live in the Parkwood Building on Shelbourne and Barrington. I was home from about ten to noon."

"Very good." He made the notations. "And what time was Yolanda here?"

"She's here all the time it seems. I know she gets here around three a.m. Most of the time she stays till closing."

"What time is that miss?"

"Six o'clock."

"She works from three in the morning until six at night?" He raised one eyebrow.

"I know, right? On Sundays, she leaves between one and three in the afternoon. I tell her she's got to hire more people. She works way too hard."

"Sounds like a good idea." He clicked his pen open and closed. "Anything else?"

Teagan shook her head. "Not that I can think of."

"Well, good day then, Teagan." He smiled at her as he walked out of the kitchen and Yolanda approached him from behind the counter. "Um Yolanda, miss, I need to…" he reached into his suit jacket and pulled out a small black business card holder, extracting a card from it. "Here's my business card. My cell and office numbers are on it. I even have an email address in case you want to contact me that way. Let me know if you learn anything else about Captain Angus Prescott's disappearance."

She took the card and looked at it. "Winston E. Churchill?!"

"Yes, miss, I get that a lot. No relation, just named after him." He shook her hand and winked. "Don't be afraid to let me know if you see anything, hear anything, or remember anything."

"Okay, Detective Churchill. And thank you."

"Thank you for the delicious energy bar."

She watched him walk quickly out of the kitchen. *He's kinda cute*, she thought.

After remembering she forgot to do the bank deposit, Yolanda took care of that and left Teagan alone to watch the yummery for about fifteen minutes. It was good to walk in the bright afternoon sunshine and feel the warm breeze. While the yummery always smelled far, far better than the dirty litter boxes she had to clean at the Crown Street Cat Shelter, she had the kind of headache-inducing responsibilities that competed with her desire to be a normal twenty-seven, almost twenty-eight-year-old, and hang out at the beach reading mystery or romance novels. Since the beginning of the year, she hadn't had two days off in a row. While BB was bright and willing as a pastry chef and helping behind the counter, she needed a shift manager once the Beverage Bar opened so that she wouldn't have to work from three AM to ten or eleven PM. A shift manager would keep BB in the kitchen where she belonged so Yolanda could train her more thoroughly, develop more new products, and refine their current offerings.

* * *

That evening she picked up her favorite Mexican dinner at Tortuga's Cafe. Having phoned in her order before leaving the yummery, she knew it would be ready for her when she got there. Once inside, she admired the old-fashioned décor of the restaurant that had been at that location for more than fifty years.

Returning home after a long day at work, she was pleased to see that Mr. Whisker and Miss Chef were in good spirits and ready for the fresh food she poured into their bowls. She set a wooden tray on her lap and sat down, glad to be off her feet. She looked forward to eating the still-hot *corn quesadilla* and *tostada grande.* Yolanda flicked on the TV and watched a romantic comedy as it had nothing to do with baking or cooking. Both cats were on the couch napping and soon she fell asleep.

Yolanda woke up, confused. The TV was still on; the cats were sound asleep on the couch next to her. Even the cushion hadn't budged from its spot against the armrest. She picked up her tray, got up and walked into the kitchen.

The cuckoo clock chimed nine times. She smiled as she watched the cuckoo peeking in and out of the small door, announcing the hour along with accompanying gong sounds. When the little bird was done and returned behind the door, on the platform below, two couples wearing dirndls and lederhosen spun around to the tinny rendition of "Edelweiss." The clock had always been in the kitchen of Lukas and Ingrid's house above the back door. It always reminded her of them. However, tonight it reminded her that she had to take a shower and wake up in about five and a half hours.

She went into the bathroom, and as she showered, she reflected on her relationship with Nigel. Having never seen his home on the border of Brentwood and Santa Monica, she'd mentioned it only last week when she was dining at an Italian restaurant on Ventura Boulevard. "Look love, it's just a house, not much to see there." She thought that was an odd response. Were they destined to remain business partners rather than potential marriage partners?

CHAPTER 4

FRIDAY

Yolanda was in her office getting caught up with all the paperwork and BB was baking cookies and making the new energy bars with a lemon curd filling topped with extra coconut. While only a sample would be offered, on Monday her new flavor of the week was going to be lemon and coconut, a lovely tart and sweet tropical combination. Yolanda reflected on how she loved to select or have one of her employees choose the flavor of the week. It was fun to alternate flavors and of course, the appreciated guests benefitted. She sorted through the invoices and noticed the Culver City address of Nigel's firm Garvey Coffee & Tea Merchants, Ltd. When would she see Nigel again? Jeannie was working until noon and Nick would cover the afternoon shift.

She pushed the curtain aside and saw that Jeannie was cleaning the front display case. There was an absence of appreciated guests in the well air-conditioned yummery at that moment, so she went out front and saw that the tips jar read:

HELP SEND MY DOG TO NON-BARKING SCHOOL!

"Jeannie, that's a silly tip of the day, isn't it?"

The older woman nodded, and Yolanda noticed her pink T-shirt and silk headband matched. Jeannie color-coordinated her work clothing. Yolanda paused for an instant, and then without thinking, she asked. "So, you know the neighborhood pretty well, right?"

"Oh yes, I've lived here for almost thirty-six years, why do you ask?" The woman stopped what she was doing and straightened up, setting the bottle of glass cleaner on the countertop.

"Um, well, I just wondered if you've ever seen Nigel's house? He doesn't live that far away from here from what I understand."

"You mean you've never been to Nigel's house?"

"No, that's weird since I've known him for almost four months, and he's been to mine. He said that it's just a house, not much to see...and I think that's really kinda weird."

"Dear me, I think that is very strange indeed. Sounds to me like he's a private person," Jeannie said.

"He's said that before. But I was wondering if you ever go by it on one of your daily walks. He's on Pacific Heights near San Vicente and Bay Drive. Like if you ever go near the place..." Yolanda looked down at the counter and then at the older woman's kindly face. "If you're ever in the vicinity..."

"I know how to play detective. I've done it before. It's better to know now then later, right?" She smiled at Yolanda.

Yolanda nodded. "Yeah, I've never had the nerve to drive by for some reason. Maybe I'm scared of what I'll find."

"Or won't find," Jeannie said.

Of course, she didn't admit to Jeannie that she'd gone on an online house tour of 14377 Pacific Heights Place as it was on the market two years ago, but the listing remained. She didn't let on that the four-bedroom, four-bathroom two story mini mansion sold for 3.4 million and that the guest house had been built in 2005. Nor did she reveal any knowledge of the area and that she'd looked at street views of his home, even though they were a couple of years out of date.

BB rushed out of the kitchen carrying a tray loaded with freshly cut samples of the energy bars. "I wonder how long this batch will last," BB said, as she transferred the bars into the empty sample tray. "The good news is that I've got a batch of chocolate chip ones in the back."

"Good girl," Yolanda said.

BB looked up as a woman with a baggy shirt and capris and gold sequined flip flops walked inside, lifting her designer sunglasses up to get a better look. "Those look good," the woman said, reaching over to grab a sample. She sniffed it before taking a nibble. "Hmmm, a bit tart, then sweet." She gobbled the rest of the sample. "I'd like a dozen of these, please."

BB stared at the woman and Yolanda explained that they would be on sale beginning Monday but if she wanted to special order them and pay half in advance, she would be able to have them ready by Saturday at ten o'clock.

After the woman made a payment, BB put the tray down and approached Yolanda. "I just wondered about that special order. It'll be made here, right?"

Yolanda nodded. "Good question. From now on, all products will be made in this kitchen, not mine. I just made the first samples in mine because they're not for sale. But from now on, everything will be made here because my personal kitchen isn't commercially certified."

For the next hour, the yummery was busy with a variety of appreciated guests and a few teens were monopolizing the tables as they ate and worked on their laptops and tablets. A middle-aged couple shared a decadent chocolate Magical Cake of Love, and he was feeding small forkfuls to the gray-haired woman who gazed adoringly at her balding mate.

BB had gone home, and Teagan strode in and informed everyone "I booked the commercial. My agent will let me know when it starts filming."

Yolanda rushed up to her friend and gave her a hug. "That's fantastic news, Teagan!"

Detective W.E. Churchill walked into the yummery. Teagan smiled at the serious looking fellow, noting his cheap brown suit and white shirt with what looked like the same necktie as the one he wore yesterday. Nope, not her type at all. She walked around the counter and went back into the kitchen, aware of the man watching her.

"Hello, Detective Churchill," Yolanda said, her good mood evaporating at the sight of him and his staid demeanor. "Would you like to try a sample of the lemon coconut energy bars?"

"Thanks, but no thanks miss. I was wondering if I could have a word with you in your office?"

Yolanda smiled. "Yes, of course."

Back in her office, the detective sat down, not looking around, focusing on her. "I'd suggest closing the door, miss."

She noted his expression and saw him taking out his notepad. "Okay, I'll do that," she said as she closed the door gently behind her. Yolanda sat at her desk, leaning forward in the swivel chair and hearing it creak. Glancing down at the desk blotter calendar, she noted the daily schedule and then looked up at the detective, as he was gazing at her. "Are you sure you don't want a cookie or..."

"No miss, I've just had lunch, but thank you. Now, have you seen Captain Angus Prescott today?"

She shook her head. "No, I haven't."

He made a note in his notepad. "I didn't think so. Unfortunately, there have been some, um, developments in the case." He flipped a page on his notepad and clicked open a pen.

"We have some intelligence about Captain Angus being in your neighborhood as recently as Sunday night. He was seen more than once last weekend."

"That's crazy. I don't even know that man except for seeing him here a couple of times a day. Why would he be in Sherman Oaks? Is he stalking me?"

"No, miss, reports have been...is Captain Angus Prescott your boyfriend?"

"No, of course not. My boyfriend's Nigel Garvey."

"Was Nigel Garvey with you last weekend?" He was scribbling his notes.

"No, I was working."

"Do you have anyone who can place your whereabouts last weekend especially on Sunday night?"

She rolled the pen so hard it fell off the desk and clattered to the tile floor. "No, detective, no one other than my cats."

"Cats don't make credible witnesses," he said, writing in his notepad. "Any human beings? Friends? Neighbors?"

"Not for Sunday night, no."

"We also have another problem. We've found the captain's jacket and undershirt in the marina floating right by his yacht. They're being analyzed in the lab as we speak. Preliminary reports suggest the substance on it is most likely blood. There are also tears and rips in the shirt that may suggest stabbing."

"That's terrible," Yolanda said. "Who would do such a thing?"

"That's what we want to know, miss."

"So do I." Yolanda said weakly. She didn't know what to say and if she said it seemed like the man had been murdered then would Detective Jump to Conclusions arrest her and accuse her of it? When talking with Detective Churchill the less said, the better. Her concerned look of a furrowed brow, which she hated doing because her mom had told her that frowning meant she'd have a wrinkled brow in her thirties.

"No miss, I have no evidence, but I want some verification that you didn't see the captain last weekend."

"Why would I? I mean, the man is like sixty-years-old. He doesn't bathe for weeks on end. He's not my type of guy. Well, my parents will vouch for me. But I wasn't with them, I was at home."

He tapped his notebook with his pen. "And where do your parents live, miss?"

"They live in Laguna Beach." She gave him their address.

"But you weren't in Laguna Beach, were you?"

She shook her head. Geez, being a detective must be a tiresome job, as you had to ask the same questions and be suspicious of people all the time. He was what her grandmother Ingrid would have referred to as a stuffed shirt. Was he like that in high school? Did he treat his classmates like suspects? He definitely needed a fancy vanilla buttercream cupcake or something, but she couldn't offer him one because then he'd think that she was bribing him.

Even though Nigel wasn't the most upfront person in the world, she really appreciated her English boyfriend.

"Well, miss, since I don't have enough evidence, I can't take you into custody." He slammed his notepad shut and put it back into his jacket pocket. "But we'll get to the bottom of this." He stood up. "Thank you for your time, Yolanda. We'll be in touch." He went over to the door, opened it, and walked out of the office.

Teagan immediately rushed inside. "Yo, what happened? You don't look so good. He didn't try anything with his handcuffs, did he?"

Yolanda shook her head. "No. But I really need an orange cupcake..."

"Will do..." she turned and left the office, and Yolanda sat at her desk, gazing at the chair that the accusatory detective had vacated. Even if the captain was wealthy and owned a yacht, the thought of dating someone older than her father wasn't appealing. Especially someone as stinky as that man. She'd been tempted to give him one of the cupcake shaped soaps she sold at the yummery's Gift Corner.

Teagan returned carrying a much-needed Valencia orange cupcake that was handed to Yolanda. "Thanks, friend." She peeled back the liner and devoured it in only a few bites. While it tasted sweet and yummy with the tang of orange, it didn't taste exceptional. Nor did it change her mood. She still felt... worried. Not like she did when she was in the throes of establishing the yummery, which had taken almost a year. What she felt now was different. A man's life was at stake. And for some bizarre reason she was a suspect.

"I can't believe the detective thinks I'm dating Captain Angus," Yolanda said as she tossed away the paper liner.

"That detective's not too smart," Teagan commented. "Especially if he thinks you're dating Captain Stinky."

Yolanda smiled at hearing the captain's nickname. "Yeah. And Nigel's cancelled another date..."

"Maybe if you drove a nicer car...or if he bought you a Porsche or an Audi."

"He's never offered to buy me anything other than dinner – and half the time he cancels. Besides, I like my car. The problem is getting enough time to see each other."

Yolanda stood up and they both left the office, hurried through the kitchen and into the yummery.

Jeannie was waiting on a pair of businessmen and chatting with a tall Black woman from the day spa at the other end of the mall. Lydia entered and Teagan waited on her and checked out the businessmen, noting their expensive suits and leaning forwards a bit to sniff the ginger-haired man's cologne which smelled so clean and fresh it was intoxicating. And the tall man resembled Prince Harry. Teagan pried him with samples and was about to give him a whole cupcake to sample rather than one of the mini ones, when Yolanda smoothly asked, "Will you be buying our six pack or a 12-pack of the fancy vanilla buttercream cupcakes, sir?"

"No thanks, mademoiselle," he said in a French accent.

Nope, not English Royalty. Teagan smiled but Yolanda knew her friend was disappointed. Although it wasn't uncommon for some people to fake accents. From what she'd read about Prince Charles's younger son, that wouldn't have been a farfetched thing to do.

But Teagan was clearly enamored with the man, prince or commoner, and grinned at him. "Where are you from?" she asked.

"I'm from Paris, France, mademoiselle. I am beginning learner of English."

"You're doing a great job. Let me throw in an extra cup..."

"Thank you, Teagan, I think maybe we can offer our appreciated guest a nice brownie," Yolanda said as she hurried over with a German chocolate brownie sitting on a wax paper tissue.

The ginger haired man bit into the brownie and rolled his narrow blue eyes that squinted shut as he chewed the brownie and then had another hearty bite until the brownie was gone and his freckled face beamed. "This very very good," he said. "I buy maybe all of them?"

Lydia purchased her usual iced tea and brownie and offered up a big smile to the men, focusing in on the ginger haired man who'd consumed the brownie. "I recommend them as well as the cookies." Lydia nodded in the direction of the tray.

"Thank you very much, good lady," the Frenchman said.

Fifteen minutes later, the Frenchman and his silent friend left carrying boxes and bags laden with brownies, cupcakes, and cookies, including several of the 6-pack cookie stacks.

Teagan stood behind the counter and watched them depart unable to help noticing the new black Rolls Royce parked in the handicapped spot. "Wow, he's hot. And mega rich! But I couldn't get his card, his name, nothing..." She watched them get inside and drive away. Sadly, Teagan looked up at the clock above the door. "Oh no, I gotta get going so I can get to work on time."

Yolanda was able to call Nick to come in for the final two hours and just as he tied his apron, an honest to gosh cowboy strode into the yummery. She stared at the man with the ten-gallon hat and saw while he wore a somber looking Armani suit; it didn't conceal the snakeskin cowboy boots with heels that added more height to his tall frame. No necktie for the lanky man; he wore a silver and turquoise bolo tie.

"Howdy, ma'am." He was looking around as the detective did, only this cowboy-hatted individual was staring more at her and the displays rather than taking in the scenery.

"Hello, sir and welcome to Yolanda's Yummery," she said, admiring his twinkling eyes and the naturally tan skin. He had a mustache and a strong cleft chin.

He sauntered up to the front counter and studied the colorful contents of the remaining cakes on one side and the last tray of brownies on the other.

"Would you like a sample of our chocolate mint brownies or a Valencia orange Magical Cake of Love?" Yolanda was aware of him staring at her intently and she felt shivers running up and down her spine. What a handsome hunka man! What a sexy Texas twang!

"Why yes, ma'am I do believe I'll try whatever sample you happen to offer me." He winked and smiled, showing off his pearly whites. "Sweets for a sweet talker, if you please."

She lifted the lid of the tray and picked out the small slice of the Magical Cake of Love and he took it from her and popped the contents into his mouth after only the briefest glance at the little cake slice in the paper cup.

He tilted his head back, looking up at the ceiling only his eyes were closed, and his mouth was moving. He then peered down at Yolanda. "Oh, my word, that cake is exquisite, and that orange flavoring is dead on perfect." He shook his head. "I know I've never seen or heard of a yummery but I just had to come in and see what was in here. And I'm glad and then some that I did." He tapped the counter. "Yes please, I'd like your last Valencia orange Magical Cake of Love and I'm sure the decadent chocolate one is just as good."

Yolanda reached beneath the counter to pull out two boxes and when she straightened up; she saw the man was staring at her as intensely as he stared at her baked goods. "That's a fine choice, sir," Yolanda said as she slid the cake from the tray into the first box with a stainless-steel cake lifter. She closed the lid and felt him watching her every movement.

"You been here long, ma'am?"

"Well, I've been here since February 28."

"Are you Yolanda?"

"Yes...I was, I mean, I could be...I mean yeah!" She smiled. "Good guess!" She giggled and tried to control her nerves.

"Well, Miss Yolanda, if you don't mind me saying this, but only a proud business owner would give me an exact date. My name's Mike O'Neill and I've moved here from Dallas last year. If you ever open a bakery like this one here in Dallas – or anywhere in Texas -- you'd have at least one hundred suitors lined up and taking numbers."

She smiled as she closed the second box and set them up on the countertop. He pulled out his wallet and removed an American Express Black Card, which he proffered with a wide grin. Oh goody, a man who paid his bills, because in order to have that kind of charge card, the large balance had to be paid off every month. Teagan loved waiting on appreciated guests who used the Black Card and was always super nice to them, especially the men, no matter what the age.

Of course, his card was instantly approved and as soon as he returned the valuable piece of plastic to his designer billfold, he scooped up the cake boxes. "No wait, I'll get you our tote bags," she said, rushing around the counter and over to the Gift Corner. She pulled two logoed beige tote bags off the rack and brought them back to the counter where she carefully added one cake to each bag. She added the small box of brownies, then picked them up and started for the door.

"Now, Miss Yolanda, I can carry those cakes all by myself," he said and gently took the tote bags from her. "And please let me pay for those bags..."

Yolanda shook her head. "Nope, they're on the house." She beamed at the handsome Texan. "Enjoy your cakes," she said.

He took the tote bags and grinned as he headed for the door. "I will do that, Miss Yolanda. And I have a feeling I'm going to be back for more."

CHAPTER 5

SATURDAY

BB was supposed to have the day off but due to the official launch of the new energy bars she was putting in her ten hours and still had three more batches of the selling-out energy bars to make. The lemon coconut flavored special order was picked up at ten o'clock and the Valencia orange and strawberry and chocolate chip bars were being sold even if people didn't try the samples.

A grandma with wavy mahogany hair walked in holding the hand of a little boy in a designer polo shirt and shorts and high tops. He made a beeline for the sample tray, which Jeannie happened to be holding. "Grandma says I gotta eat glutee free stuff. You got any?"

"We certainly do, young man," Jeannie said, bending down to offer him a chocolate gluten-free energy bar. "I hope you like chocolate!"

"Raymond loves chocolate, don't you Raymond? Now tell the nice sample lady thank you!"

"Nice sample lady, thank you!" He reached for the small piece of chocolate covered granola, grinned, and quickly bit into it. "It's good."

"Do you want me to buy one for you honey?"

"Yeah! Mommy says I can eat all glutee free stuff 'cause I don't go like this..." The boy put his wrists in front of his mouth and blew loudly, making a noisy farting noise that caused Yolanda to giggle and Jeannie tried not to laugh.

"Well, that's nice to know!" Jeannie said as the boy continued to make farting noises.

"Raymond, honey, I think we get your point. Now stop it and let's buy some of these for you and your mommy."

When there was a brief lull in the early afternoon, Yolanda and Jeannie were back in the kitchen cutting up the energy bars and filling the cookie stacks. Nick was going to work until closing so they were doubly relieved to have him there. He put up a new sign.

LEAVE YOUR CHANGE WITH US – THANK YOU!

He was in a great mood, having had a strawberry bar, and was praising them to the hilt and showing off his energy saying he would've gotten higher scores in the *Need for Speed* video game which made a family with two pre-teenagers' new fans of the bars and of the cookie stacks.

Yolanda took the freshly cut chocolate chip energy bars and neatly arranged them on a tray. Jeannie was cutting the Valencia orange bars and looked at her work rather than at Yolanda. "I did find out some news about Nigel yesterday evening," she said.

Yolanda looked at the woman, noting her serious expression. "Yeah? And?" She paused, awaiting the news, feeling her stomach clenching along with her fists.

"I don't know the whole story, of course, just what I saw. I happened to be taking a little stroll down his street. And I saw Nigel." She cleared her throat. "But he wasn't alone."

"Was he with another woman?" she asked, knowing that Jeannie didn't like to tell people bad news. Once a customer's credit card had been declined and Jeannie offered to pay for the Magical Cake of Love.

"Unfortunately, he was. She was very young, I'd say early twenties, blonde, and they both had those suitcases with wheels."

"And I haven't gotten a text or email or anything from him since he was here on Thursday morning! Where were they going?"

"From what I could see it was her car. It looked like a new black Mercedes."

"Do you think it was his sister? I know he has a sister. No, wait, she's older than me, she's in her thirties."

Yolanda looked crestfallen as the realization washed over her. *He was another cheater. Was that all men did was look for any available woman in their early twenties? She was already in her late twenties and was increasingly less desirable. Just because he had a British accent and came from money didn't give him the right...oh it did so*, she thought. *He was young and handsome enough to be deadly sexy to most women, he was wealthy, athletic, and he was a cheater.*

Yolanda picked up the tray of energy bars and went out into the yummery to add them to the almost empty tray already there. So, what if he was a cheater, she knew she wasn't and she was also lucky enough to have her own yummery. There were nearly a dozen people crowding around trying samples and buying her concoctions. How many of them had been cheated on?

She had just placed the last bar on the parchment paper lined tray and happened to look up as the front door opened. In walked Detective Churchill. She smiled at the gray-suited man, as though he was one of her spendier appreciated guests. As she was miserable about Nigel's extracurricular girlfriend, oh no were they off to Hawaii or the South Pacific? Suitcases usually meant travel...But she had to appear calm and collected and look and act like the "up and coming entrepreneur" that she was.

Detective Churchill approached the counter right where she was standing. He looked at her, not at any of the free samples or at the goodie-filled display cases that attracted most normal people's attention. "Hello Detective Churchill," she began, "Would you like to sample our new chocolate chip energy bar? They were just made ten minutes ago." She smiled through her internal pain and the sight of the suspicious man who made her feel like a suspect.

"Hello Yolanda. Can I see you in your office?"

No, because I'm not in my office I'm standing right here you darn fool. Some big deal detective you are if you can't tell the difference. "Yes, of course," she said. No reason being snotty to the man—probably preferred junk food anyway. Oh, and doughnuts. Lots of greasy fried doughnuts and cheap coffee. Yolanda was so glad she didn't make and sell doughnuts.

Back in her office, they resumed their seats – he in front of her, she behind her desk trying to appear calm and composed.

"Miss, there are some new developments with the Captain Angus Prescott case. It would be best if you could come down to the station and discuss it there. It's more private that way."

"I can close the door if you'd like."

"No miss, I think it'd be better if you could just come to the station. We're located just off Santa Monica Boulevard, and you'll want to go to...."

"Excuse me, detective, but I have a yummery to run and I'm debuting a new product today as well as the fact that Saturdays are the busiest day of the week and if you want to talk we can talk here for about..." she glanced at her watch. "I can spare five minutes."

His eyes narrowed and he fixed his cold gaze on her. "I hope I don't have to take you into custody to get you to answer some questions and discuss some facts. This is now a very serious missing person case---and it could be a murder case. You're entitled to have a legal representative accompany you."

"Why would I need a legal representative? I have nothing to hide. I'll be down there within the hour as there are some things I must take care of right now."

After he left, she closed the door behind him. What a crappy day. First the Nigel situation, where he was hanging around with a younger woman. Now she HAD to go down to the police station. Well, at least she wasn't being handcuffed and dragged into a police car, but even so, she still had to go somewhere she didn't want to go—and soon. *Better sooner than later because later turned to never*, her grandfather Lukas used to say. Yeah, right. She wished she never had to go down to a police station. She automatically reached for her desk phone to call her mother. Just as she was about to hit the speed dial, she stopped and hung up. Better not worry her parents over nothing. She was innocent and she knew that she had nothing to hide. In fact, she could be the bigger person in such a situation. Maybe she could use her Magical Cakes of Love. No, that was too obvious. However, a few brownies, cookies, and cupcakes...oh, and maybe a dozen Valencia orange energy bars...

After indulging in a chocolate mint brownie and only feeling a slight nudge of euphoria that vanished almost immediately, Yolanda figured that her afternoon wasn't about to improve noticeably.

The drive to the station only took ten minutes and she didn't have any problem finding a parking spot on a side street.

She sported her yellow logoed T-shirt and carried her purse and a large pink canvas tote bag filled with goodies. Smiling, she made her way into the station, surprised at the coldness of the reception area as well as the noise and all the people. As she approached the uniformed police officer behind the reception desk, Detective Churchill suddenly appeared from the hallway on the right and nodded when he saw her. "Good afternoon, Yolanda. Please follow me."

Friendly, as usual, she thought, as she walked quickly behind the detective down a long hallway bustling with activity. She saw he was carrying a bulky file folder. A muscular uniformed officer with a nametag reading Aikens smiled and looked at her tote bag. Churchill turned around, noticed the other man staring at Yolanda, and cleared his throat. "Yolanda, let's go into this interview room."

"Interview? For TV? A magazine?" Yolanda looked at the detective while the uniformed police officer smiled at her.

"Yes miss, though most people think of interview as a job," he smiled at her. "I assume you already have a job?"

"I'm the owner of Yolanda's Yummery in Brentwood." She opened her bag and pulled out a yellow cellophane bag of cookies. "Do you like oatmeal raisin?"

He licked his lips. "Miss, I love oatmeal raisin."

"Good! Here you are," she handed him the brightly tagged Yolanda's yummy 6-pack cookie stack which he opened and proceeded to grab one and shove it into his mouth. He shut his eyes and his face relaxed, and he smiled and swallowed the cookie and chuckled. "Best um, darn cookie I've had." He looked at the hangtag and nodded. "Oh, I've heard about this place saw something online about it."

"Right, thank you Officer Aikens. But I have an interview..." Churchill lifted his eyebrow, and his half smile wasn't convincing.

"Well, expect to see me next week, Miss. Mighty fine cookie you bake." He gave her a quick salute and hurried down the hallway.

Just as Detective Churchill unlocked the door, a frizzy-haired woman in a beige pants suit rushed down the hall. She stopped a few feet away, noticing the tote bag and squealed "Yolanda's Yummery! My sister got one of your magical love cakes for her birthday and she met her fiancé! I heard they're awesome!"

"Would you like to try some cookies or brownies?" Yolanda asked.

"Ladies, I have to interview Yolanda...and not about her cookies," Churchill said.

"Oh, boo hiss, Churchie, you're so boring. Can I try one of your brownies? Please? How much are they?"

"Free for anyone at the West L.A. division today," Yolanda said, reaching into the tote. She opened a bag and extended it to the woman. "Let me get you a napkin," she said.

The woman reached into the bag and picked up a brownie. "Thanks, but no thanks, this'll be gone in a jiff..." she inhaled the aroma and then took a good-sized bite. She chewed briskly. "Um, yum, I see why it's a yummery!" The woman finished and walked away, giggling. "Thanks so much!"

"You're welcome!" Yolanda waved and smiled at the departing woman.

Detective Churchill and Yolanda sat down inside the empty room with a large conference table. They sat across from each other, her tote bag on the table. He stared at the logo.

She reached inside, pulled out the bag of brownies, and opened it. Instead of the acrid stench of sweat and poorly circulated air conditioning, the aroma of chocolate nut brownies wafted in the detective's direction.

"Care for a brownie, Detective Churchill?" Yolanda asked.

"I'm the one doing the interviewing here, miss."

She picked up a brownie, so it was between them, the tantalizing chocolate scent even stronger. "Your loss. If you won't, I will." She reached into the bag, pulled out a small stack of napkins, and set them on the tabletop. Removing a brownie, she set it gently on the white surface. Now they both gazed at it, a perfect square of intense dark chocolate loaded with chopped California walnuts. "That's right, detective, I use locally grown nuts..." she smiled.

He couldn't resist—the smell, the lovely lady across from him dressed in her bright and perky T-shirt that showed off her assets, but most of all that chocolate walnut brownie fragrance only inches away. He reached for it, unable to resist the lure of the brownie. "Well, if you insist...I love chocolate and walnuts local or foreign..." Churchill picked it up, looked at it closely for a few seconds, and took a bite. Two more quick bites later, it was gone. "Thank you, miss. It's...superb."

She grinned. "Quite the compliment."

"Umm hmmm," he nodded and opened his file folder. "So did Captain Angus Prescott enjoy your brownies?"

"Yes he did."

"Did he ever sample them?"

"Of course."

"Did he sample them at your house last weekend?"

"No, he didn't. He sampled any and all of my samples at the yummery."

"Were you two involved?"

"No, not at all. He was an appreciated guest. Of course he ate samples."

"But not at your house on Willowbrook Street in Sherman Oaks?"

"Nope."

Detective Churchill looked at the top sheet of paper in the

folder. "We received an anonymous tip that he was at your residence last weekend. You two were seen together."

"That's impossible. I told you; he wasn't there. I have no interest in the man whatsoever.'

"That's not what I heard."

"I have a boyfriend. Nigel Garvey. He's twenty-five. The captain's what—fifty? Sixty?"

"He's fifty-eight. And very wealthy."

"Teagan would be interested in him if she knew he was rich."

He looked down at the folder and flipped a few pages over. "Your employee, Teagan Mishkin?"

Yeah, my employee and good friend. He really had the hots for her, but she thought he was some poor crazy guy. If she'd known he really was rich...and owned a yacht..." Yolanda noticed his intense look. "But she didn't."

"Well, again, I say you and the captain had some close involvement. Because why would he write this?" He pulled out a scrap of notebook paper and showed her the five words: "Yolanda Carter is the best"

She shook her head. "I have no idea."

"We also discovered a comb aboard the captain's yacht. A comb with a few long brown hairs in it. We'll need a hair sample to compare yours to see if it matches."

There was the sound of pounding on the door along with the jiggling of the doorknob. "Hey, you almost done in there?" A loud voice asked.

"Hollis, we don't have any doughnuts in here," the detective replied in an even louder and more annoyed voice.

"Got any cupcakes or brownies?" Hollis asked.

"I've got brownies..." Yolanda said.

The door burst open and a tall lanky man in uniform stormed in, "'scuse me but Aikens told me about the cookies and Sylvie said the brownies are to die for...police humor, miss... and I just thought Churchill here would let me in for just a sec."

The interview ended after Yolanda donated a few strands of hair to a technician who also tried one of the chocolate walnut brownies and asked for a business card. And on the way out of the station she gave away another cookie stack and two more brownies to some of L.A.'s finest.

After the yummery closed, Yolanda went into the kitchen and assembled the ingredients for the next day's cookies and energy bars. That way, she wouldn't have to arrive at three in the morning and she could show up around six in the morning instead. It was also BB's day off and she knew she had to hire an employee who could at least mix the ingredients for them, run the dishwasher, and do basic food preparation. Also, the construction crew wasn't working that weekend so she could bake in peace. She was able to work faster than usual, as there were no interruptions. Pop music blared from the speakers. Tomorrow she'd have the afternoon to herself. Only it would be spent at home making the fondant cake decorations for Rosemary's upcoming wedding.

By nine o'clock, it was almost dark outside, and she'd finished all the prep work, even down to scooping the cookie dough onto the parchment sheet-covered trays. Storing everything in the walk-in fridge was going to make starting the next day's baking a breeze. The dishes needed to be washed and she put all the bake ware and mixing bowls and utensils into the commercial dishwasher. She flicked on the switch and walked away from the big machine and headed for her office. The phone rang. Who was calling after hours? Instead of letting it go to voicemail, she reluctantly answered it.

"Yolanda's Yummery."

"Hey Yo, I'm outside," Teagan said.

Yolanda went over to the stereo and switched it off. "Outside where?" she asked, looking around.

"The yummery!"

Yolanda hurried into the yummery and saw her friend standing there waving at her. The young woman wore dark shorts and a crop top. Black platform shoes completed the ensemble. It looked like she had been working at the Wicked Fun Gentlemen's Club. But things hadn't gone well for Teagan as her cheeks were streaked with mascara.

She rushed over and unlocked the front door, stepping aside to let her friend in. "Teagan, what's wrong? What happened?" Yolanda locked the door behind them and in the front part of the yummery they stood, Teagan weaving slightly with emotion and a lack of stable footwear.

"It's been a terrible day, Yo." The tears flowed and she cupped her hands to her face to hide the obvious fact.

"Teagan, what's wrong?" She gave her friend a hug.

"I was arrested and went down to the …"

"Arrested?" Yolanda stared at her friend in shock and pulled away.

Teagan pulled her hands away from her face and looked down at the floor. "Well, it seemed like it. Detective Churchill stormed into the club and demanded I go back to the station with him for an interview."

"Did you go with him in his car?"

"No. I went down there after he left. I didn't have a choice. And Rocky fired me."

"Your boss fired you?"

Teagan nodded. "And it couldn't happen at a worse time. I don't have a boyfriend and I really need the money. I'll have to sell my car."

"But why did he fire you?"

"Can't have cops showing up at the club demanding

dancers leave in the middle of their shifts. Bad for business. That's what Rocky said...but he was getting sick of me and my auditions..."

"Let's go back to the kitchen and talk about it. I have some oatmeal raisin cookies left or if you wait about ten minutes, I can put a few chocolate chip cookies into the oven..."

"I'm fine with oatmeal raisin. And some milk too, Mom."

They went back to the kitchen and Yolanda pulled out a plastic wrap-covered tray of oatmeal raisin cookies from the shelf. She peeled back the plastic and let Teagan select her cookie. The distraught young woman grabbed one and promptly bit into it.

"Ummmm, this is so good. Now where's the milk?"

Yolanda smiled. "I'll get it." She walked over to the fridge and pulled out a pint and handed it to Teagan.

She untwisted the top and took a long gulp. She sighed. "Nothing like milk and cookies. Makes me wish I was a kid again." She sighed. "Of course, having lots of money would make me feel younger and better. Like being able to shop at Tiffany's again, and not have to look at the price tags at Neiman Marcus..."

"Yeah, I know what you mean. Back before we had to be interviewed at the police station." She paused. "I think it used to be called interrogated..."

"Interview. Interrogation. Different words same meaning." She took another swig. "Saturday night and I'm drinking milk! Wow you're such a bad influence, Yolanda."

"If it wasn't for me you wouldn't have gone down to the police station," Yolanda said. "I'm so sorry for saying you like rich men."

"But it's true. I love rich men."

"Just not Captain Angus, right?"

"Yeah. I mean, the whole point to being rich isn't to hide it by looking and stinking like some homeless guy. It's like driving the best car, wearing the best clothes and living in the best house."

"You're right. But I know that you and I both want him to show up again. Even if he doesn't look and act like a millionaire."

CHAPTER 6

SUNDAY

Yolanda returned home by one-thirty, and she changed into a turquoise tank top and shorts. Her cats were delighted to see her and after she gave them some turkey treats, she found some colorful wool balls she had needle-felted and tossed them around. Miss Chef grabbed one with a graceful jump and her paw got stuck in it for a few seconds. Mr. Whisker slapped it away from her, picked it up with his mouth, and ran down the hallway. "Now be fair, Mr. Whisker," Yolanda said. She tossed another wool ball in Miss Chef's direction and the cat grabbed it with her front paws and began rolling around on the floor with it. Yolanda smiled at the sight of her cats playing.

She sat on the floor and opened a cabinet so she could pull out all the containers of rolled fondant icing. There were also little jars of luster dust and supplies that she'd need for creating decorative flowers and stars that would be added to the wedding cake. She pulled out containers of dragees and pearls in purples, blues, and frosted whites. There was a pastry wheel, small rolling pin, assorted flower-shaped stamps and little plastic cookie cutters that stamped the designs. All the cake creator accouterments were placed on the quartz-topped island.

Yolanda carefully arranged them, so the colors were in one area, and in another were the decorations. The sound of a car pulling up along with three short taps of the horn made her smile. She put down the silicone mat and then turned to go to the back door.

A cobalt blue Toyota Prius was parked in her driveway and her mother stepped out of the car. Her auburn hair was in a messy bun and with only lip gloss and minimal eye shadow, the woman looked much younger than her fifty years. Dressed in peach-colored capris, a matching shirt and white sandals, the outfit showed off her athletic frame. Her father wore his usual flip-flops and baggy surfer shorts along with a green T-shirt; ordinary work apparel for the Laguna Beach-based glass blower. He stepped out of the car holding a large clear glass cookie jar with thin swirls of pink, yellow, and mint green.

Once inside her house, he passed the work of art over to her. "Guess where this color combo came from?"

She beamed as she accepted the beautiful creation from her father's large hands. As she held it up to the sunlight streaming in from the window above the sink, the glass shone in the afternoon light. "It's amazing, Dad!" It was carefully placed next to the cake decorating supplies. "I hope you sell lots of these. I'll need a few for my shop."

He smiled. "Got three more in the car. Two with the company's colors and a clear one. If anyone asks, I can do other color combinations."

"Dad, it'll look great in any color."

"Dear, do you have any lunch plans? I mean, other than working?" Abby pushed the little plastic rolling pin back and forth.

"Nope. Nigel's not coming over today and ..."

Abby stopped rolling it and shook her head. "Sounds to me like he works more than you. If that's even possible."

Yolanda wondered if she should tell her about the scenario in front of his Brentwood house that Jeannie had reported on. Instead, she decided not to ruin the beautiful sunny afternoon. "Yeah, I guess," she smiled to avoid any further discussion about her Nigel-less weekend.

"So, who wants a picnic?" asked Abby.

"Are you kidding me? I can't say no to that!" Yolanda exuberantly replied.

"Great! Let's get the picnic hamper..."

They walked out to the car and Frederick removed the large woven hamper while Abby reached into the back seat and pulled out the 1960s red and white Coleman jug. The sound of ice cubes sloshing around made Yolanda smile. She knew that her mother's special sun-brewed black and green teas loaded with fresh lemons and a few scoops of sugar was in there and it was her favorite drink in the world that her mother made. The insulated jug was from her grandparents, so they were bringing it to the original home. Yolanda reached in and grabbed the red oilcloth tablecloth and a bag of condiments, and the happy family walked into the backyard.

Beneath the orange tree was the old-fashioned wooden picnic table that Yolanda bought last year at a yard sale. It was something she'd always wanted.

Frederick unfurled the tablecloth and then placed the big basket on top of it, flipping the top open. Abby fussed over unloading the plates stored in the lid along with the utensils.

"How does homemade chicken and rice sound?" Abby asked as she reached into the basket and began removing the lunch. "Sometimes I just don't feel like eating imitation meat!"

Yolanda chuckled. The memories were unfolding as her mother unloaded them. Warm cornbread, coleslaw, hummus, and gluten-free pita bread. And for dessert: sweet ambrosia fruit salad. The whipped cream base was loaded with marshmallows, fresh pineapple and Mandarin orange chunks, shredded coconut and sliced maraschino cherries. It was beyond sweet. Her mother called it a *splurge dessert,* and everyone in the Carter family was a big fan.

Frederick removed cups from the basket. Setting the jug on the edge of the table, he placed a cup beneath the spigot and pushed the button. Yolanda watched the stream of sweet golden iced tea pour into the cup. Her father handed it to her, and she sipped the cool beverage, the sugary and tart lemon taste mingled with the blend of teas. It reminded her of the camping trips they took when she was a kid and they sat at a picnic table much like the one she had now. Usually it was in a tree-filled area and the drone of insects was heard in the distance. She recalled the woodsy smell of the Redwood Forest and the other state and national parks they had enjoyed visiting.

Her mother plated the first course and as soon as the chicken hit the plates, both cats came out of hiding in the bushes and hurried over to investigate. They were galloping in unison, both of them exclaiming in Catinian *oh look it's chicken time!* Miss Chef's jade green eyes and Mr. Whisker's coppery green eyes stared at the feast. Yolanda pulled off some slices and fairly distributed them to her feline friends who gulped them down with gusto. Miss Chef finished first and sat on the grass looking adoringly at her. Just as Yolanda was about to donate more of her meal, her parents contributed a few pieces so there was enough chicken to go around. The cats ran over to the corner of the yard and hid beneath one of the bushes. Soon they'd be having their afternoon siesta.

Yolanda enjoyed her lunch, drinking two cups of iced tea and smothering her corn meal muffin with butter that she brought out from the kitchen along with a couple of strawberry energy bars for her parents to eat later. The sugary and fruity ambrosia was pillowed with whipped cream and fluffy marshmallows that she had loved since first tasting it as a preschooler.

The picnic table was near the side of the yard and the white picket fence was only about three feet high, so she saw the tropical print sundress-wearing Mrs. Steele stroll past. When the older woman turned and saw the family, she waved, showing off the undulating flab in her arms. "Hi Mrs. Steele," Yolanda said brightly, and the parents echoed her.

"Hello!" the older woman answered and continued, rounding the corner so she was walking past the side of the Carter cottage.

"That woman would benefit greatly by doing some upper body exercises. The plank position would be extremely helpful," Abby commented as the woman slowly made her way along Willowbrook Street.

"Good luck with that. She does a daily walk around the block and gets winded."

A black and white police cruiser rolled down the street and slowed down, then stopped at the stop sign. There was a significant pause as though the driver was demonstrating how not to do the California rolling stop. Then it continued along, and seconds later stopped again. Yolanda paused, her fork a few inches from her mouth. She watched the car as it drove along at the speed of Mrs. Steele—*slow, far too slow*, she thought.

Frederick and Abby had their backs to the house and couldn't see the street as they sat across from her. "What's wrong?" Frederick asked.

"This cop car is just sitting in the middle of the street now," Yolanda said. "That's weird."

Suddenly it swung into the driveway and parked behind her parents' car.

Why was a police car pulling into her driveway on a Sunday afternoon?

The car doors opened, and two uniformed police officers stepped out. Both wore standard uniforms and sunglasses. The driver of the vehicle was chubby and had a reddish complexion. The man emerging from the passenger side was tall and lean. Behind the two men, another black and white unit suddenly appeared at a faster rate of speed and when the second vehicle stopped, the brakes squealed. The second car parked in such a way as to block the sidewalk.

North on Willowbrook Drive raced a black Ford sedan that parked to the side of the driveway, right where Yolanda's trashcans went every Tuesday morning. The person getting out of that vehicle was a grey-suited Detective Churchill. He strode up the driveway and over to Yolanda and her family. "I'm here to issue a search warrant on 12790 Willowbrook Drive. This is the home of Yolanda Carter?"

"Yes it is," she said, staring at the young detective.

"Ma'am, we have a search warrant to search the premises for information obtained from an informant in the missing person's case of Angus Prescott."

"What in the blue streaking blazes does this have to do with my daughter? Let me see that thing!" Frederick stood up.

Detective Churchill showed the search warrant to the father. "Sir, this warrant was signed by Judge Evans this morning at 11:15. He takes these cases very seriously, as do I. It appears that Miss Yolanda Carter has been in the company of Angus Prescott last weekend."

"That's not true! I was working!" Yolanda piped up. "He's an appreciated guest at the yummery, I've told you that."

"Yes you have. But I have an informant who claims otherwise."

"You're serious?" Abby voice was shrill with surprise. "How on earth do you think my daughter has anything to do with that man?"

Detective Churchill looked at the search warrant and held it up. "Ma'am, this is what I go by. Judge Evans signed it this morning, so that's good enough for me."

"I still don't understand what any of this is about," Abby remarked.

"I'd suggest you talk with your daughter about it. Now if you could stay here while we conduct the search...oh, and we're going to have to access your garage and your car."

Yolanda glanced at her garage and then back at the detective. "My car or..."

"Your car, Miss Carter," the detective said abruptly.

"Yolanda, are you going to tell me what's going on here?" Abby said as the detective and accompanying police officers walked back to the driveway. "This just isn't something I've seen except on TV."

"Mom, all I know is that one of my appreciated guests has gone missing. Captain Angus used to come in twice a day...you saw him at the grand opening, the homeless guy with the captain's jacket."

"Sure, I remember him..." Frederick said. "But what do you have to do with a missing customer?"

"Nothing. But the detective seems to think we're involved!"

"What?" exclaimed her parents in unison.

"Detective Churchill says that there's an anonymous tip that the captain was here last weekend."

Abby shook her head. "That's beyond ridiculous. You were working..."

"Dear, even Yolanda doesn't work 24/7...though I think it's pretty close," Frederick remarked as he rubbed his beard. "I don't understand why they think some homeless guy would be over here."

"He's an heir to the Prescott fortune. He's really rich and lives on a yacht in Marina del Rey. The detective said they found my hair in a comb on his boat. Yesterday, I gave him samples of mine to prove it wasn't. I don't understand how the samples could match."

Abby went to the picnic table, refilled her daughter's cup, and brought it back. "Dear, maybe you should have some more iced tea."

Yolanda shook her head and stared gloomily at the cottage as she watched the five cops enter through the back door. The sight of them going into her home was unnerving and the sudden loud crashing noise made her jump. She headed towards the driveway, followed by her parents. Just as they reached the kitchen door, Detective Churchill blocked their way.

"It might be a good idea if you'd wait out here in the driveway or on the sidewalk," he gestured to his right. "And we'll also be searching the garage and your vehicles', so it'd be easier on you if you unlocked your garage and vehicles."

"Now wait a minute," Frederick said. "Why the heck do you need to search my car? And yes, I know, it's on the property."

"Sir, you've just answered your own question," the detective said coolly, raising an eyebrow. "Leave everything as is in the backyard. We'll make this as quick as possible."

The sound of something metallic hitting the kitchen floor made them all start. Her parents supported their ashen-faced daughter. For an instant, Detective Churchill looked at her with widened eyes, as though comprehending her distress. He gave her a curt nod and said, "No one likes to have their homes searched. If it's any comfort to you, these men are all experts, they've done this thousands of times..."

A loud voice from inside called out: "Hey Church, you gotta see this!" The voice was growing closer along with the heavy footsteps. "You gotta see..." the chubby cop stopped as soon as he saw the Carters.

Detective Churchill turned towards the uniformed older man.

"My bad, uh, detective, we need to see you inside..." The chubby cop cleared his throat. "Uh, we..."

"Higgins, that's enough. I'm right behind you." The detective turned and followed Officer Higgins back into the kitchen. The cuckoo clock chimed three times. Everyone was startled by the unexpected interruption. Yolanda knew the performance began with the cuckoo peeking in and out of the small door, announcing the hour along with accompanying gong sounds. Officer Higgins and Detective Churchill went inside and stared up at the clock. Now that the little bird was done, on the platform below, two pairs of dancers wearing dirndls and lederhosen spun around to the classic folksong: "Edelweiss." After it was finished, the men shut the door and the Carters headed towards the sidewalk.

The Carter family standing on the corner of Dove and Willowbrook were the objects of many stares. Mrs. Steele was in her front yard wielding her hose as she needlessly watered her blossoming yellow and pink rose bushes. In her other hand she held a cumbersome old cordless phone up to her ear as she loudly chatted. "Selma dear, we have THREE police cars on the street right outside the Carter Cottage!" She paused, spraying the overwatered roses and furtively looking at the yellow house on the corner. "I've lived here since 1965 and I can't remember the last time I saw anything like it on this street. Certainly not when Lukas and Ingrid were living there. What is this neighborhood coming to? No, no, it's..." she noticed Frederick and Abby glaring at her and turned her back on them, almost tripping to the ground in the process. The garden hose fell and sprayed her, and she dropped the phone, yelling as it fell to the soft grass.

A beefy man in a tight polo shirt and skinny jeans, walked

by with a well-groomed collie. The excited dog strained at the leash, sniffing and barking. The man held the leash, but the strong dog tugged mightily and got loose, still barking and eagerly following a scent trail. The dog sprinted up to the sidewalk-blocking police cruiser, the long nose surveying the back wheel, and emitted some cries. The dog raised his hind leg and began relieving himself. The owner hurried up and grabbed the leash, yanking the dog away. "Now that's not nice, Sergei," He chided as they walked away.

The unhappy family waited outside the cottage. They followed the progression of the search, hearing voices and noises as the premises were being ransacked. Frederick reached for his cell phone. "It's time to call Kyle Newman," he said, turning on his phone and flicking through his contact list. "He's our lawyer," he patted his daughter on the shoulder. "Don't worry, this guy really knows his stuff." He wandered over to the side of the fence closest to the driveway.

As her father waited to speak to the man who'd solve the increasingly complicated problems Yolanda was undergoing, she thought of all he had done for her over the years. On her fifth birthday, he taught her to ride a pink two-wheeler, running up and down Sunny Glen Drive, always within reach, so he caught her before she fell off the bicycle that wobbled underneath her shaky balance. Eleven years later, he handed her a key that unlocked a new yellow Honda Civic, allowing her to drive to school instead of riding the bus.

She watched as he covered his ear with his large hand and pressed the slim phone up to his other ear. He wasn't into technology and didn't use any hands-free devices. His hands were attuned to creating delicate glass sculptures and cookie jars, cake stands and jewelry. She'd watched him in his studio twirling molten hot glass and changing it into *objets d'art*. Or he'd twist a long pliable tube of glass into small intricate beads which would form necklaces or bracelets.

A muffled thud sounded from the living room region. More people from the neighborhood ambled along, some local guy from the other side of the street shuffled by a cigarette hanging out of his mouth. As Frederick was involved with listening to the lawyer, Gary the neighbor gawked at the cop cars, and Yolanda saw the cigarette was unlit. *How weird to walk around like that*, she thought.

"Hey Yolanda," Gary said. "Looks like you got some company."

"Hey Gary, just my parents."

The man looked around "...yeah, and the media."

A white Channel 12 news van pulled up and parked at the corner behind the detective's car.

Meanwhile, Frederick was still on the phone, unaware of the van. "Okay, Kyle. Thanks." He disconnected the call and pocketed his phone. He looked over to watch the goings on. There appeared an older man with an orangey-red toupee that contrasted with sparse silver hair fluttering around his ears. Paired with a burgundy plaid jacket, sky blue shirt and matching tie, the ensemble was finished with gray slacks and loafers.

For an instant, Yolanda stared at the man's funky attempt at color coordination. Was he dressing for the Clown Channel? She recognized Vern Hess, the man who had interviewed her former boyfriend, Zac Field, just after winning the 25th Annual Green Palms Mini Golf Tournament. And she remembered how Zac had publicly kissed a young blonde fan with enough passion to cause the reporter to tell them to get a room at a motel. The incident happened over a year ago, and she had moved on to Nigel. Zac had moved on to a series of girlfriends, according to him. Now he also worked part time at a golf shop in West L.A. His main source of income was being employed as a golf pro at the Green Palms Mini Golf Course. Selling equipment at the golf store, he hoped to snare more investors in his scheme of building the Biodome Valley Mini Golf Course in Simi Valley.

Vern grinned and began his patter. "This is Vern Hess with Channel 12 Action Street News. I'm here on a quiet residential street in Sherman Oaks outside this quaint little yellow cottage. This is the home of Yolanda Carter, the young proprietor of Yolanda's Yummery in Brentwood. I'm not here to sample one of her award-winning brownies or her romantic Magical Cakes of Love. I'm here to interview her for the disappearance of fifty-eight-year-old Angus Prescott, also known as Captain Angus. For those of you who don't know your movie history, and shame on you, Angus Prescott is the sole heir to the Prescott Moving Pictures empire. He is the grandson of George Prescott, the founder. His father, George Junior, was the famous Hollywood movie producer from 1936 until his death in 1971. He won many best producer and best picture awards over the years. In fact, *Whoa Nellie* is one of my favorites!" He whinnied like a horse.

The reporter grinned, clutching the mic, and the athletic looking camera operator was focusing on Yolanda's startled face. The reporter pivoted and approached her. "Yolanda Carter, this is Vern Hess with Channel 12 Action Street News."

He moved a few feet away and gestured for her to follow. She reluctantly did so, standing closer to the edge of the driveway.

"Can you tell me when you last saw Captain Angus?"

"I think it was Sunday afternoon."

Vern smiled. "Ah, so you admit to seeing him last weekend."

"Yes, at the yummery. As I told Detective Churchill, he always showed up twice a day – once in the morning at seven when we open, and again around three in the afternoon. He was a greatly appreciated guest."

"So do you think he's missing – or dead?"

"Why, I hope it's neither one of those. That would be awful."

"Yolanda, how long were you and the captain lovers?" Vern edged a little closer to his interviewee.

"We weren't lovers," Yolanda said. "He was an appreciated guest. That's what I told the detective and now I'm telling you the same thing. He …"

Frederick stepped over and reached for the mic, but Vern pulled away.

"I think we're done here, Vern," Frederick stated.

Abby went over and stood next to her husband and daughter. "Yes, Vern. I think we're done here. My daughter's a pastry chef and she has nothing to do with the disappearance of the captain."

Frederick held his wife and daughter's hands and the family proceeded to turn and walk back up the driveway and approach the kitchen door.

Detective Churchill stepped out, closing the door behind him. Before he said anything, the chubby red-faced officer brushed past him, a trace of crumbs on the side of his mouth. "Excuse me, miss, but I couldn't resist one of your fine chocolate chip cookies…it was excellent!" He beamed, his face deepening in color. "I need to stop by your bakery."

The detective stared at the cop. "You know you're not supposed to take anything from the suspect's property. Only evidence. And I don't think a chocolate chip cookie is evidence in this case. Maybe evidence of your sugar addiction and lack of willpower."

Frederick looked at Yolanda and then back at the detective. "Did you say my daughter's a suspect?"

Churchill nodded. "I'm afraid so, sir. We found a pair of the captain's underwear in her laundry hamper. Also, a bag with a tin of Astleys No. 2 mixture, an imported pipe tobacco. The Dunhill estate pipe is estimated to cost over one thousand dollars and that, along with the tobacco, was found in her china cabinet. And five thousand dollars in cash in her car's glove compartment."

Two more officers passed them and returned to their cars.

"What? I never have that much in cash in the house or car. I mean I keep about forty dollars and some spare change inside the center console..."

The detective opened the kitchen door and nodded for them to enter.

Yolanda stared in dismay at the mess. The fondant supplies were shoved to a corner of the island and small containers were on the floor – along with some of her silicone bake ware. Every cabinet door was flung wide-open, displaying haphazard stacks of dishes in one cupboard and a disarray of canned and boxed goods in another. Many of the items were overturned or cluttered the countertop and floor.

Her heart pounded so loudly she thought everyone in the disheveled kitchen heard it. There was so much cleaning up to do. So much unnecessary straightening up and returning everything to its correct location. She was furious at the invasion of her home and all her baking, cooking and food items being displaced. And for total strangers to be stomping around on her clean floors while wearing their dirty shoes.

Just then, the other two police officers entered. Higgins looked at her, then down at the floor. "So sorry, miss, but I just had to try one of your cookies. Best I've ever had."

Detective Churchill glared at him. "Next time do Yolanda the courtesy of buying cookies at her yummery..."

The police officers departed.

"I'll get to the bottom of this. I always do. I don't figure you for a gal that smokes imported tobacco out of an expensive pipe...but we've got the evidence and we'll run the tests on it. Same with the captain's shorts." He shook his head. "Facts can be mighty strange things, miss. But that's what I work with." He looked around. "It looks bad and there was a vase in the hallway that broke, sorry to say." He shrugged. "We try to be careful, but shh...um, stuff happens." He was carrying a black briefcase. He walked to the doorway. "By the way, miss, make sure you don't leave town. I'll be in touch. Soon. Goodbye." Detective Churchill opened the door and departed.

The parents returned to the kitchen and the family stood next to the messy island and looked around the room again. Frederick headed into the dining room and saw the breakfront china cabinet's doors and drawers open and his mother's tablecloths lying on the floor. He was about to retrieve them when he noticed the curtains were open. He strode over to a living room window and peered outside. "Holy moly!" he shouted. "Girls, look at the crowd outside!" He stood aside as his wife and daughter went over and had a look—gasping in disbelief. Two more news vans from competing local stations pulled up along with a large cluster of nosy pedestrians. There was also more traffic along both streets. The doorbell rang.

"Don't answer it," Frederick said as he reached over and closed the curtains. "Make sure all the curtains are shut."

They raced around the house and closed curtains or mini blinds, encasing the cottage in gloomy darkness. Outside, they heard the noise of slamming car doors, people conversing with one another and milling around. Some of the local looky loos were being interviewed by reporters. The noise was disruptive as it sounded like a street fair had overtaken the once-quiet neighborhood. A furtive glance out of the mini blinds showed Mrs. Steele happily yammering into a mic a reporter had thrust near her double chin. "I've known them since…well, Lucille Ball was on TV!"

Abby and Yolanda returned to the kitchen and began cleaning up the fallen bakeware. "Mom, I'll take care of the kitchen and my room, okay?"

"Sure honey," Abby said. "Maybe I'll do the guest room. And dad will take care of the living room and dining room."

"Sounds like a plan." She began the task of straightening out her kitchen.

Several hours later, the family was exhausted from reorganizing drawers and closets, vacuuming carpets and washing floors. The damage assessment was small, a broken vase from the hallway table and a lamp in the guest room with a dented shade.

In the guest room, they stood, looking around. Abby reached down on the desktop and picked up a miniature felt figure of a tuxedo cat that had fallen over. She smiled and put it on top of the computer monitor that covered most of the white desktop. "I'm glad your Aunt Margie introduced you to needle-felting," she said.

Yolanda looked at it for a second. "I'd forgotten about that. I need to make one that looks like Mr. Whisker."

"And our cat, Carson. Did you use only wool roving?"

"Nope. I got some alpaca on sale, and it feels even smoother." She went over to the desk and bent down, opening the bottom drawer. "That reminds me, I've also done miniature cupcakes." Going through her felting supplies, she pulled out a plastic bag filled with bright colored fibers. "I even use sari silk and bamboo to add texture and shine." Handing her mother the bag, the woman opened it and pulled out a tangle of shiny silk in vibrant primary colors, along with a colorful strawberry-topped cupcake.

"Wow, you're really good at this, Yolanda." She pulled out

another one with brilliant shades of orange. "Really good, dear. Maybe you can sell these?"

She took the small imitation cupcake from her mother and held it up to the lamplight. "Oh, I forgot, I sometimes add stellina and firestar. It's like glitter but it comes in long strands."

Abby fished through the bag and pulled out a bunch of glittery white and blue fibers. "That's so cool."

"Artists," said Frederick. "I'm glad you're so talented, daughter. Being an artist helps one get through the rough times."

Abby handed the bag to Yolanda and went over to the doorway and switched off the light. She glanced at the activity outside which had lessened as the media had departed. Several people still lingered about the area on the warm night.

"We're not going to leave you alone like this tonight." She stepped away from the window, gently tugging on the mini blinds to make sure they were shut. She sighed. "It's not safe being here alone." Abby hugged her daughter. "What a mess."

"Don't worry mom, we'll be fine. We always have each other."

Frederick walked into the room and embraced his wife and daughter. "Yes we do."

CHAPTER 7

MONDAY

It's a blue Monday, Yolanda thought, unable to sleep. At one-thirty, she gave up trying and got up. She debated about whether to wear a pink, yellow or green T-shirt to work. She wished that she'd chosen navy instead of a cheery yellow as part of her color scheme. It matched her mood on that dark first day of the workweek.

Arriving an hour later, she saw the lights on in the future Beverage Bar, noting the addition of the long counter, the three workers were diligently putting together. Two more weeks until that opened. Gil Resnick waved at her as soon as she shut the door behind her. "Saw you on the news last night," he said. "I say that dumpster diver's an old fool. Heir to a fortune and he acts homeless? You know last week he hit me up for spare change? A multimillionaire asking me for money! Now that's rich." He laughed.

"It's strange that's for sure," Yolanda said, heading toward the kitchen, not wanting to talk but work.

Gil nodded, not wanting to work but gossip with the pretty young suspect. "I can't see you and the captain dating. Don't look like your type."

"He's not. He's an appreciated guest. That's all he is. If he has the money, he can buy what he likes. Maybe I should say, only from the yummery cases..." Yolanda said.

"By the way, what's this week's flavor?" asked Gil.

"Lemon coconut. Also, we have the new energy bars."

There was a loud knock on the front door and Yolanda turned to see BB standing there waving and smiling. She rushed over to unlock the door and let her pastry chef in.

"I'm so glad you're here, Yolanda. I saw you on the news last night and that reporter was really asking some dumb questions."

Yolanda locked the door behind BB. "Tell me about it."

"Your parents are great. I like how your dad said to that reporter the interview was over."

"Yeah, my dad stands up for me. He's like that," Yolanda added.

"I wish my dad was like that. He doesn't do much of anything but drink beer and watch TV. Ever since the truck accident he just ... well, at least he was good for taste testing anything I made," BB remarked. "He didn't mind doing that."

Yolanda snickered and the two of them walked back to the break room.

BB wore her yellow shirt and apron that contrasted with new black jeans. She peered into the other building and saw the young carpenters working on the now u-shaped wooden bar. "Hey Lance, hey Pepe," she called out.

They looked up and grinned when they saw the brightly dressed pastry chef. "I'm wearing yellow because we're doing lemon and coconut flavor of the week," she told the men. "We'll be having some sweets for you pretty soon."

"Thanks, BB. That's awesome 'cause I love me some lemon," Lance remarked.

Pepe smiled and nodded in agreement. "Yes, I love lemon."

For the next three hours, Yolanda and BB cranked out the new energy bars, cookies, cupcakes and Magical Cakes of Love in the perky flavor combination. She was grateful to work as it helped her stop thinking about her recent problems.

Until the first morning break, when the carpenters gathered around to sample some cupcakes and cookies and Gil opted to have a lemon coconut energy bar. "Let's see if this new energy bar of yours works 'cause I'd love to stay awake longer when the sun's out."

Yolanda handed him one and he bit into it and smiled. "Now this is so gooooood!"

Yolanda let Jeannie inside and noticed a dozen or so people milling around the sidewalk in front of the yummery. A few cars were pulling into the parking lot from San Vicente Boulevard, including two news vans. She locked the door behind Jeannie.

"Good morning, Jeannie, you're early."

"Hi Yolanda. I couldn't sleep. I was so worried about you. I saw it on the news last night."

Yolanda sighed. "That's the problem with bad news, it sure gets around fast. Doesn't matter if it's true or not. Geez, I have no idea why the captain's missing."

"Neither do I, dear. But I just don't see the two of you as a couple. Especially as Nigel is far younger and handsomer."

"You got that right. Though I have to get to the bottom of who that mystery woman is..."

Among the early arrivals at the yummery were the regulars including the Goldbergs, Lydia Sloan, Clarabelle and her mother, Dani Kramer and many others. It was a busy morning, as Yolanda had to do two more repetitive interviews with a couple of morning shows. The questions and answers were the same. However, the woman reporter for Channel 1 took a shine to the lemon coconut energy bars and told the viewers to try them out, so she got extra free publicity. As soon as she finished, she called in her parents, Nick, and Teagan as reinforcements. Nick arrived within the hour looking frazzled from lack of sleep as he was working on a new psychology project. However, he found the time to print out an amusing tips jar sign that read:

MOO! MOO! MOO! - COWS CAN TIP – SO CAN YOU!

"I was gonna say boats can tip but because of the situation with some missing yacht dude, I figured I should change it," he commented to Jeannie. "I think we'll get lots of tips today…" The young man gestured at the line that was snaking through the yummery and back out the door.

Abby and Frederick wore matching yellow aprons and T-shirts when they arrived at noon. BB was the only one in the kitchen doing the baking as Yolanda was alternately helping behind the counter or answering the incessantly ringing phone, mostly fending off interview requests. Even when the Other Patrick Stewart showed up, Yolanda wasn't quite as gracious towards him as she had been in the past. She consented to do an interview, but it was very brief, except for promoting her new flavor of the week and the energy bars.

BB managed to leave an hour after her usual quitting time, so Yolanda was baking more cupcakes than usual, followed a close second by the new energy bars. Upon her mother's insistence, just after three o'clock she was finally able to take a lunch break that would do double duty as a lawyer's meeting. A block away was Jimmy Janga's a Tex-Mex restaurant that had an outdoor patio setup in the back with tall latticework fencing interwoven with ivy that offered some privacy. The name was a play on the word *chimichanga*, which was a deep-fried burrito.

She was shown a table near the corner and was relieved to see several empty tables in the immediate vicinity. She was given a glass of water and handed a menu by the smiling young hostess in a ruffled dress. A slight man in a charcoal gray suit rushed over to her table. "Yolanda Carter?"

"Yes I am. Are you Kyle Newman?"

"That's me," he had a big grin and extended his hand, showing off manicured nails. When they gripped hands for an instant, she was surprised at how soft his skin felt.

Well, he's a lawyer, she thought.

Short brown hair slicked back and blue-green eyes showing faint laugh lines; the skin white and freckled, an indoors type.

They consulted their menus and ordered the same thing: the special of the day: Jimmy Janga's stuffed with jumbo shrimp and tossed salads. They opted to drink water even though she noticed him eyeing the extensive *Cervezas* section. No drinking and driving for Kyle Newman.

From the briefcase he placed on the chair to his right, he pulled out a file folder and set it in front of him. "Now, I've got to warn you this is a high-profile case due to the Prescott name. That means you're under scrutiny – as you already know. It's also been a week since the captain's been seen and the evidence linking the two of you together. I know what you've said. But whatever happens, know that you have 100 percent confidentiality with me."

"I'll tell you what I told the detective and the reporters – the captain was an appreciated guest, and you know that means nothing more than a paying customer. I don't see how anyone would think I had a romantic interest in that man – I have a boyfriend. Um, sort of."

He nodded as he paged through the papers. "Your sort of boyfriend is Nigel Garvey of Garvey Coffee & Tea Merchants Ltd. Based in London. He's lived in the States for the past four years."

"Right. We've been dating since March."

"Not very long. And I see the name Zac Field…"

"What does he have to do with this?"

"You tell me."

"Nothing. I haven't seen him in at least a month…maybe two? He's a nice guy but all he does is play miniature golf."

"Well, no matter. It seems that there are people who want this case solved very quickly. The man's been missing for seven days now. Over the weekend, the evidence found in your residence has linked you two together even more. The D.A. may upgrade this to a murder investigation due to the discovery of the captain's intimate items in your home. Plus, the evidence of your matching hair samples found aboard his yacht. What I need to know is this – did you do it?"

"This's ridiculous. I have no interest in the man. I didn't date him, I didn't go to his yacht, and I couldn't even imagine killing him. I don't kill."

"I admit you certainly sound convincing, Yolanda Carter. And by the way I must try some of your yummery's yummies…" he stared at the logo on her chest for a few seconds. "Now, I tend to believe my clients," he winked. "However, I need to warn you that my services don't come cheap – especially for this type of case. If charges are pressed it will be very expensive to defend you. We're talking six or even seven figures."

"Six or seven figures? I'd lose the yummery for sure…" she stared at the ivy-covered fence to her left.

The waiter returned with the food, which was made into a production of serving, as each plate was perfectly centered in front of the diner and the imperious looking man made sure they had all the needed condiments. When he left, Yolanda gazed down at her plate with the hearty rolls of nourishment contained within the corn tortillas stuffed with jumbo shrimp, rice, sauces and cheese. Her belly growled as she'd only had one energy bar that day, so the sight of a full meal was tempting.

He smiled at her. "Go on, eat, you'll feel better. Myself, I haven't eaten since six."

Even lawyers are human, she thought, plunging her fork into the plump Jimmy Janga.

"Now, before we talk more about the money side of things, I want to tell you the most important thing you can do – or can't do. Don't talk to the press, and don't talk to the cops unless I'm there. Next time a reporter waves a mic your way the only two words you need to say are: no comment."

Yolanda gave him a half smile and nodded. "No comment. Easy to remember."

"Make sure you do. I've had too many clients ruin it by yammering on and on. One of them was convicted and sent to San Quentin because of it. So, please heed my advice and don't comment."

"Okay." She looked up and saw a hefty round-faced man with a thin smile on his flushed face made his way over to their table.

"Hey there, I'm Sam Fleming. I'm a representative from Freeze N Bake. You that Yolanda Carter babe?" He leered at her, staring at her shirt.

"No comment."

Kyle laughed. "Fast learner, I like that. My name's Kyle Newman, of Jenkins, Newman & Fleiss in Beverly Hills. How may I assist you, um, Sam?"

"I'm talking to the little lady, here, mister." Sam wove a bit closer to her, still staring at her chest. "Well since you got a lawyer maybe we can ink a deal. We buy your yummery and all your recipes, especially that brownie recipe and…those magic cakes."

Kyle stood up and dropped his fork down on the plate with a clatter. "Look, Sam, you're interrupting us and if you don't..."

Sam turned and looked down at Kyle. In addition, Kyle was reaching into his breast pocket and pulling out his cell phone. "Um, okay..." he staggered off back to his table on the other side of the patio.

"You handled that very well, Yolanda."

"No, you did. Thanks, Kyle."

"You're going to find out real fast who your friends are. I hate to say it but it's true. Adversity like this really tests you. Personally, I think you are innocent on all charges. And I intend to prove it." He glanced at his cell phone and frowned. "Well, time to go. I'll call you tomorrow after I learn more...oh and I'll buy lunch."

"Thanks, Kyle," she said as he quickly left to take care of the bill.

For one block, she was able to walk alone down the sidewalk and she paid no attention to the honking horn of an oncoming car. A huge SUV heading in the same direction veered towards the curb, the horn sounding loudly and the shout of "killer..."

Was Kyle right about the charges? Had they escalated from missing person to murder? She shook her head and hurried back to work. She hadn't been remotely interested in the captain and now this -- being called a killer on a public street? One thing was certain; whoever had shouted that out was severely misinformed, as her father would say.

As she approached the Brentwood Grove Shoppes mini mall, it was obvious that business was booming going by the full parking lot and the addition of three news vans parked near the yummery. *Not what I need to see*, she thought. Walking past the parking lot's entrance, she heard the beeping sound of another car horn. Refusing to look, she marched on, determined not to let any insults affect her.

"Yolanda! It's me, Teagan!"

She turned and saw the ruby red Mercedes sedan and her friend behind the wheel, the window rolled down, her hand waving. "Yolanda, big news!"

"What's going on?" she leaned forward and looked inside the import with the black leather interior smelling of saddle soap and an undertone of a musky and piney smelling cologne. In the passenger side sat a big muscular man with a black ponytail and goatee.

"Yo, let's go talk in your office. But I need to find a parking space."

"Okay," she said as the tinted windows slid up and the car made a turn down the first aisle.

Yolanda was able to utter "no comment" several times to various reporters, including Vern Hess.

"Yolanda," he said, trying to move closer to her. "We hear the case may change from a missing person to murder. Now I covered the O.J. Simpson case right here in Brentwood and…"

Yolanda kept on walking until she was inside the crowded yummery.

Before she returned to the office, she checked on the goings-on and saw the stock was approaching an all-time low especially for two hours before closing time. She rushed into the cooler and found a dozen freshly frosted lemon coconut cupcakes courtesy of BB's last batch, along with two dozen plain brownies that had been made that morning. She smiled, grateful that BB was such a responsible employee.

Back in her office, she sat behind her desk while Teagan and the burly guy drank coffee and feasted on brownies. Only Teagan was drinking coffee as the man was already on his third brownie and to Yolanda's concern wasn't showing any signs of slowing down.

He's eating into my profits, she thought, noticing the

muscular upper body packed into a tight black short-sleeved top. His biceps were huge. She wondered how much food he put away.

Teagan watched as he downed his fourth brownie. "Yolanda, this is Salvatore Ferrera, a/k/a Tank. He's a P.I. and has friends all over L.A. both cops and the Mafia..."

"There is no such thing as the Mafia..." he crumpled up the napkin and tossed it into the small wastebasket near the doorway. "Ah, that's a joke. Two points!" He raised his beefy arms over his head at the successful shot.

"Tank says both you and me need his help. They're nosing around me, and they were outside my apartment this morning. Now we hear it may be called murder...that's unbelievable from someone who worked in a no-kill cat shelter for three years."

Tank smiled. "I used to have a cat, but he ran away...nice animals but can't train 'em."

"Some are more trainable than others," Yolanda said.

"My friend Teagan found two cops nosing around outside her place this morning. Ask me, I say cops are only there when you don't need 'em."

"So, what do we do?" asked Yolanda.

"Go down to Mexico," he said.

She smiled. "I was told that's not an option."

"Lemme guess, that Churchill guy told you not to leave town, right?"

"Exactly."

"Then maybe we need to go down to the marina ourselves and take a look at the captain's yacht."

* * *

That night, before going on their mission, Yolanda went into her office, opened her earthquake preparedness kit, and removed two flashlights for her and Teagan. Both young women wore black jeans and tops, courtesy of Teagan. Her friend also brought along plain black baseball caps. Yolanda glanced at her watch. "We absolutely have to be out of here by nine-thirty—night construction crew usually gets here by then."

Teagan nodded. "Okay. And maybe you should park two or three blocks away. Not near my place 'cause Tank thinks it'll be under surveillance…"

"Good to know. When will he be back?"

"Any minute. Let's go," Teagan said.

As they left the yummery, Teagan gave a quick glance at the Gift Corner.

"Too bad you don't have anything black without a logo on it."

Yolanda smiled as they walked out the front door and locked it behind them. "Yeah, suddenly I regret all these pretty pastels and the advertising of my business. Who'd of thought?"

Teagan said, "You had no way of knowing." She paused, looking at the entrance. "But take a look at that steamer ship." A long car glided up to the curb near where they stood. Teagan smiled at the glossy vehicle. "It's almost as big as a limo."

The midnight blue 1972 Buick Electra 225 with a thick coating of carnauba wax and shiny chrome fenders and rims shone beneath the lights.

"My dad would adore this," Yolanda said, admiring the classic car.

The passenger side window rolled down and Tank smiled at them. "Ladies…adventure awaits in the Electra Lady…"

Inside the massive car, Yolanda sat in the supple leather back seat even though there was enough room for all three of them in the front.

He flipped on his DVD player and the soothing sounds of

the Charlie Parker Quintet oozed through the many speakers inside the luxury car.

Thirty minutes later, the car pulled into an almost full parking lot next to a sprawling Marina del Rey apartment complex near land's end. He shut off the ignition and swiveled slightly in his seat to address them. "Now put on your caps and leave 'em on. Walk and talk quietly," he lowered his voice. "Out here sound really carries. Those may be yachts but they're about a foot apart in the slips. Above all, don't turn on any lights in the captain's yacht. Use these..." he flicked his mini flashlight on and off twice. "Any questions?"

"What are we looking for?" Yolanda asked.

"You'll know it when you see it. Basically, anything that proves your innocence. Now leave your bags here. We're going in to grab and go...we don't want to be there for more than a few minutes. Lots of security out here with such boats."

After getting out of the old-fashioned car, Tank led the way and the fresh night ocean air hit them. Yolanda noticed he was wearing all black apparel and had added a thin windbreaker. They approached a narrow dock, and the big man gracefully and lightly strode down it. Yachts lined both sides of the passageway above the water, and the intermittent creaking noises made Yolanda more vigilant than ever. Staring at the ocean from her Laguna Beach home and walking along the shoreline was the extent of her aquatic expertise. California-born and bred; she'd only been on a boat once back in sixth grade on a family outing to Catalina Island. Halfway through the thirty-two-mile trip she got seasick. The unpleasant sensation departed as soon as she landed on the small island. But the thought of the return journey which would provide another bout of seasickness made it the worst day trip ever.

Near the end of the dock, they stopped in front of the Sunseeker yacht named *Whoa Nellie*! Yolanda covered her mouth to keep from laughing. But the yellow plastic Police Line – Do Not Cross tape at the boat's entrance knocked away her amusement upon seeing the corny name.

They ducked beneath the tape and stood aboard the deck of the slightly rocking 75-foot yacht. Yolanda shivered in her thin top as a gust of wind caressed her. Being on the surface just above water and not on land was disconcerting to the yummery owner.

Tank stood near them and whispered, "Pull out your flashlights and keep 'em away from any porthole."

"What?" Yolanda and Teagan asked in unison.

"Windows," Tank replied tersely. "Follow me below deck into the saloon."

Going down a curved stairway with elegant carved railings led them into a plushily carpeted room. The trio of flashlights showed off what appeared to be a sumptuous living room. A pale leather sectional couch, a large wall mounted TV and in the corner was a dining area with a modern round table and matching velvet chairs.

"Wow, it's hard to believe a homeless guy lives here," Yolanda said.

"I know, right? I could get used to this," Teagan said, running her hand across an elegant velvet overstuffed chair.

"Ladies, lights down, voices down, and start looking—and not at the scenery. We need clues." He paused. "Follow me," Tank said.

"It stinks like tobacco," Teagan said sniffing the air and waving her hand in front of her nose. "I remember he smelled like it whenever he came into the yummery."

Down a narrow hallway lined with expensively paneled teak wood walls and into the captain's study with the same paneling. Beneath a porthole sat a multi-drawered desk. Tank reached over and closed the curtains, darkening the room. He concentrated the light on each drawer that he opened. Yolanda took one side of the drawers and rifled through the contents. Teagan was assigned the smaller center drawer. As Tank reached the bottom drawer, he discovered a shoebox at the very back. Opening it, a sheaf of papers filled the box. Quickly flipping through the contents, he called out in his stage whisper: "Storage locker bills." He flicked through the rubber-banded stack and lifted them out of the box. "Okay, this is a good lead. Now where the heck are the keys?" He returned the box to the drawer and removed a plastic Ziploc bag from his inside jacket pocket, shoving them inside and closing it.

They searched the built-in bookcase next to the desk. "Wait, I've got a hunch," Tank said, squatting and pulling out a handful of hardcover sailing and nautical history books. He reached back with his paddle-sized hand, first right, then left... and removed a ring of keys. "Okay, now we're getting somewhere." He pocketed them.

Just as he stood up and was about to leave the office, he saw a blinking red light. Next to the phone sat an answering machine. "Jiminy Cricket, this thing must be fifteen years old," Tank muttered. He pressed the PLAY button. A perky woman's voice said: "It's date night! I'm on my way over. I'll pick up some things from the deli."

Yolanda paused when she heard the feminine voice. There was something familiar about it. Audible background noises consisted of ringing phones and voices along with the clatter of fingers on keyboards. An office? The second message was similar. "Hey lover, it's me. I'm on my way over and will stop at your favorite burger place and get a double cheeseburger and fries and your chocolate shake." The last message consisted of the same woman announcing the fact that she was going to pick up a smoked turkey on rye.

Yolanda shook her head, "I've heard that voice somewhere…"

A loud noise outside the yacht startled them. A man shouted: "There's lights coming from the Prescott yacht! Call the police!"

Tank lowered his flashlight as he led the young women out of the yacht.

Fleeing out of the harbor, Tank took them on a whirlwind ride around the circuitous streets of Marina del Rey until he pulled up to a small restaurant at the edge of Santa Monica: Emilio's Italian Kitchen.

"Okay, ladies, dinner's on me, my treat." He parked the car in the alley behind the restaurant and walked in the back way. "I know the owner," he said as an explanation.

As soon as they walked in, a rotund older man wearing a black designer suit shuffled over to Tank.

"*Ciao, Salvatore*!" he said, reaching over and the men kissed each other's cheeks.

"*Ciao, Emilio*!" He put his arm around the older man and spoke in a low voice. Then he brightly said, "These are my young lady friends Teagan and Yolanda." He gestured and the restaurateur eagerly kissed and hugged them, especially Teagan. Teagan grinned at the man, looming over him so she saw his bald spot.

"So, we can have the private room for a little while?" Tank asked.

In a cigar-scented private room furnished in rich burgundies and golds, they sat at a linen-covered table, feasting on chunks of olive oil-sprinkled *ciabatta* bread, and shared a large deep-dish Sicilian pizza. After inhaling several slices, Tank removed the stack of bills and the key ring.

"Let's play match 'em up." He moved his plate and laid out

the bills on the tabletop. There were fourteen of them. Tank counted only seven keys.

He studied the addresses on the bills. "Looks like we got Hollywood, Burbank, Sunland, Culver City, West L.A., mid-Wilshire, all over. Fourteen storage units, but only seven keys."

"I wonder what's in all of them?"

"If I had to guess, I'd say guns, drugs, and maybe stolen merchandise." He returned the keys to his pocket and bundled the bills back up. "I'll get some guys to look at these storage lockers." He winked at Teagan. "Never really know what we'll find till we get 'em open."

Chapter 8

Tuesday

Nigel showed up at the yummery wearing a navy tracksuit and running shoes that morning. Surprised to see him in non-business attire, Yolanda left the crowded yummery and led him back to her office. She closed the door behind them and slumped back into her chair.

"Honestly, Yolanda, you're not looking too good," Nigel said.

"Thanks for telling me something so obvious," Yolanda replied. "This morning when I got here there was no construction crew. Gil called and said starting tomorrow they'll be working the six to two shift because of his schedule," she whined.

"Well, my lady, it's like this. Next time hire someone who'll stick to the schedule."

She sighed. "I guess, but I thought he was reliable."

"As long as the work's getting done and hopefully will be completed on schedule. This affects my business too, you know." He paused. "I really don't want to hurt your feelings, Yolanda. I know you're a very nice person, but, well..."

"This isn't sounding too promising."

"Probably not. I just want us to maybe evolve into an open relationship—see other people," he gestured with his expressive hands. "I mean, all this must be so very stressful for you."

"And you don't want to hang around me because I'm practically a murder suspect now, right?"

"Well, no, not exactly. But, well, maybe. It's..." he fumbled to get his thoughts in order. "This isn't easy for me, you know."

The phone rang. He took that as a suggestion to leave and she didn't stop him as she answered it.

* * *

Her mother arrived at ten to help behind the counter and Teagan was scheduled to work along with Nick that afternoon. BB was working the six to six shift that day due to the need for more sweets in the afternoon. It was during a brief lull awaiting the cookies and cupcakes to emerge from the ovens, and only a few appreciated guests enjoying their treats, when BB tentatively approached Yolanda in her office.

"Um, Yolanda, is it okay if I talk to you for a minute?"

Sure, BB, what is it?" Yolanda closed the recipe book she was compiling and felt her stomach twist into a knot. She couldn't afford to lose BB.

"Well, as you know, I used to work at the county fair every summer," the teenager began. "And I used to do fudge demonstrations," she said.

Yolanda almost burst out laughing in relief. "Yes, it was on your resume."

BB smiled. "It was so much fun to do. I got pretty good at it too."

"I bet you did," Yolanda smiled encouragingly.

"We called it the Fantastic Farmer's Fudge demo. I made all kinds, plain chocolate, chocolate walnut, my favorite, chocolate mint, my second favorite. Even strawberry, vanilla, pistachio, peanut butter...it kinda depended on the day of the week. Anyway, I was wondering if maybe this fall, maybe in October or November, you'd like to do something like that? Like maybe in the Beverage Bar if there's enough room?"

Yolanda nodded. "I've made fudge before. I know you need a marble surface, and it helps to have a copper kettle. Gosh, I think it sounds like a great idea. Because fudge is yummy no matter what time of year, but I think you're right about it being more of a fall treat." She made some notes on a notepad. "I'm definitely going to look into this. Thanks so much for suggesting it, BB."

The young employee's round face was flushed with happiness, and she hurried back to the kitchen to remove some trays of cookies from the oven. Yolanda was about to check into the price of the fudge making equipment when the phone rang. She quickly answered it seeing that it was Teagan. Listening to her friend, she nodded. "You'll be right over." She paused, listening closely. "A storage unit in Hollywood? Oh, okay." The call was disconnected. Yolanda took off her apron, grabbed her purse and closed her office door.

Once in the yummery, she pulled her mother aside and whispered in her ear that Teagan was coming over, but they had to leave for a couple of hours to check something out and would return well before closing time.

Yolanda took the freeway and exited at Western Avenue, making slow progress as she headed north. Teagan wore another toned-down outfit and was nervously playing a game of solitaire on her cell phone. Once Yolanda turned onto Santa Monica Boulevard, she saw the Hollyview Cemetery and parked along a side street north of the boulevard. She set the car alarm and left it, looking back at the new car once, scouting the low-income neighborhood comprised mostly of multi-story apartment buildings and ramshackle houses divided into several rental units. Four preteens were playing soccer on the street and a smiling Hispanic woman walked by holding a white bakery box from the nearby *panaderia*.

In front of the Hollywood Starz Storage facility, they spotted Tank's gleaming vintage car and he stood near it along with another bodybuilding type, a bald man sporting numerous tattoos on his skull, neck, chest and arms. Tank introduced them to Chopper, who eyed both women with obvious interest, especially Yolanda in her pink T-shirt. "Are you Yolanda and are you yummy?"

"No, she's the owner of the yummery – it's like the best kind of bakery ever," Teagan said.

"Who am I to argue?" Chopper nodded. He grinned and shook their hands. "Now ladies, do you know about the legend of Hollywood Starz Storage?"

Yolanda shook her head.

"Um, no," said Teagan.

"A couple years back, someone spent some time in one of the third-floor storage units."

"Hey, let's go inside and you can tell it on the way up." Tank led the way to the side door entrance and the other three followed.

"Okay. How long they spent in that unit, no one knows for sure. What they do know is that this person got away with six million dollars in cash."

"That much?" Yolanda asked.

They walked down a hallway that led to a pair of elevators. Tank pushed the up button. They waited.

"That much, maybe more. No one knows for sure. It was stored in some boxes. All of it in cold hard cash. Tax free. There's a bounty on that bastard's head..."

The elevator dinged and slowly the doors opened.

The foursome boarded the large steel elevator.

"It's a sad story, but not for the person who got the cash. If they still got it, that is," Tank said. "So, now what happens here is..."

Yolanda and Teagan watched as the doors closed with equal slowness and the elevator lurched upwards. They looked at Tank.

"The man who runs this storage place says that the captain's storage locker was unloaded today. He saw a woman and two moving men wearing green uniforms with a Summerfield Moving Company van parked in the loading area. They cleared the unit out. We need to see if anything's left in the unit." Tank said, watching the number finally change to three.

"How would you live in a storage unit?" Teagan asked. "I mean, how would you go to the bathroom? Take a shower?" She shook her head.

"And there's no view," Yolanda said.

The doors unfurled in slow motion, and the ladies stepped out onto the concrete walkway. They saw long rows of numbered corrugated doors. The place was as silent as one of those mausoleums in the cemetery across the street.

"Good thing I'm not wearing heels," Teagan remarked, as the concrete floor echoed under their footsteps.

"Over there. Number 362-J," Tank pointed.

Clustering around the storage unit, they looked at the lock. Chopper pulled out a small piece of iron. "Allow me to open it," he said as they dispersed.

Yolanda nervously watched. "We're breaking in. I may have

a murder charge over my head and we're breaking into a storage locker."

"Relax, Yolanda," Tank said. "The owner doesn't care if we do this. We paid him not to say anything..."

"Got it!" Chopper exclaimed as he grabbed the lock before it could noisily fall to the floor. The big man reached down and rolled the door up like a small manual garage door.

A flick of the light showed that the unit was almost empty. In the rear corner sat a toppled space heater in front of a couple of old standard letter-sized boxes. Tank walked in and lifted the dented box lid. It was half full of eight by ten headshots of actors from the 1950s and '60s. He thumbed through them, seeing many were signed in heavy black or blue ink. "Dorothy L'Amour, Tad Hunter, Michael Landon, Biff Wellesley..."

Yolanda shook her head. "Isn't Michael Landon from the *Little House on the Prairie*?"

Tank nodded. "Yeah but this was around the time *I was a Teenage Werewolf* came out – 1957. But I've never heard of Biff Wellesley."

Chopper shook his head and went over to the second box, carefully removing the lid. "Holy crap! Look at all memorabilia in here!" He gently pulled out a stack of various-sized booklets and the titles dated back almost forty years. Movie titles flipped past: *The Poseidon Adventure*, *The Towering Inferno*, *Earthquake*, *Airport*, *Jaws*, *Car Wash*, *Harold and Maude*.

"Guess the captain collected this stuff," he exclaimed, looking at promotional booklets and early media kits that the studios and productions companies sent out.

"Is it worth a lot of money?" Teagan asked.

"Yeah, lots. And no telling what they took. Collectors go bonkers for this kinda stuff. Like shoes worn by an actor in a movie, props, costumes, even personal things like passports and drivers' licenses. Captain's dad and granddad knew everyone from Marlon Brando to Cary Grant to John Wayne. Thing is, the longer they're dead the more that stuff's worth."

Tank said, "Whoever took this is after the captain for all his memorabilia. If all fourteen lockers are filled with movie memorabilia, it's worth a fortune." He glanced at a signed headshot of Lucille Ball. Suddenly his cell phone rang, startling everyone. Tank pulled it out of his pants pocket and quickly left the unit. As he listened to the caller, he paced back and forth down the empty hall. A minute later, he disconnected the call and pocketed the phone. When he returned to the storage unit, his face looked stressed. "Yolanda, I'm afraid it's not good news. Stan is one of my police buddies and he's Churchill's supervisor, so he's involved in the case. CSI determined that the hair they found in the comb on the yacht is yours. The pipe and tobacco is the captain's – his fingerprints are all over it. The boxer shorts are his and they have his DNA on record due to some problems in the past, um, so it's a match. The worst news is that the DA wants to file murder one charges."

"But I..." Yolanda couldn't finish her sentence because she collapsed to the floor of the storage unit.

Teagan screamed and went over to her fallen friend's side. She patted her face. "Yolanda, get up! Wake up!"

Yolanda stirred, her eyes closed, head rocking back and forth. "No, no, no I didn't ..." She opened her eyes and looked around. "Why am I on the floor?" She shakily tried to get up and Teagan and Tank helped her. Teagan reached into her purse and pulled out a water bottle. "Here, it's a new one," she handed it to her friend.

"Thanks," Yolanda opened it and took a sip. She paused and took a gulp. "I've never fainted before."

"With news like that, I know I would have," Teagan said.

"I'm gonna keep digging into this, because it's interesting. I want to know who's behind this," Tank said as he reached into his waistband and removed a small gun, checking the ammo.

"Me too," said Chopper, pulling out his weapon from his waist and doing a quick inspection on it.

"Oh my," Yolanda said, almost dropping the water bottle. Chopper reached over and supported her for a few seconds before letting go. "This is gonna get hairy," he said. "But I suggest you resume your normal duties, like they say…"

They were back at the yummery at three-thirty. Teagan quickly changed into her uniform and Yolanda tied on her apron and was brought up to speed by her mother as they sat in Yolanda's office.

"Mom, I just can't figure all this out. I'm a nice girl. I barely know the captain. And now I'm a murder one suspect!"

Abby shushed her daughter. "It'll be on the news soon enough, don't say anything, just do your job."

"Yeah, that's what Chopper said."

Abby raised an eyebrow. "Who the heck is Chopper?"

"Chopper and Tank are helping me with the case," Yolanda said.

"Chopper and Tank? What kind of people have names like that?" Abby shook her head. "Wait, don't tell me. Just know that your father and I are here for you. If you'd like, we can spend the night with you again."

"Thanks, Mom. It's okay. This should all blow over soon." She went into the kitchen where BB had just put more trays of lemon coconut energy bars on the rack.

Helping behind the register, she was relieved to see that the afternoon crowd was clamoring for her sweet treats, including the popular energy bars. Two lemon coconut Magical Cakes of Love were sold by Teagan. A group of a dozen women from a nearby office building were chatting and sampling some cookies. The line near the front of the yummery had several people in it who were either texting or talking on cell phones. As she restocked the energy bars, she overheard a woman's voice that sounded familiar. It wasn't a famous person, not a singer or an actress…it sounded like the voice on the answering machine she'd heard the night before. Was it one of the office workers? A random customer? She listened carefully but then her phone rang, and she answered it.

"Yolanda's Yummery," she said.

"This's Tank. The remaining storage lockers have been checked. In all cases, it's been a woman with two men from the Summerfield Moving Company. They cleaned out the lockers. Found some left-behind movie memorabilia."

The steady stream of appreciated guests continued until almost closing time. To her surprise, Zac Field walked in, and she saw the look of concern on his face. He wore a kelly green polo shirt and tan chinos. "Hey Yo, I'm on my way over to my pro shop job," he said.

"Hey Zac, good to see you," she said, and meant it as they walked to the back of the yummery near the refrigerated beverages. She slid open the door and handed him an iced tea. "On the house."

"Thanks, Yo." He shook it, uncapped it and took a long swallow. "Hey, I want you to know that I think you're innocent. Whatever happens, I'll stand behind you."

She gave him a quick hug. "Oh, thanks so much, Zac. That means a lot to me."

"I know you don't have a mean bone in your body. And I also know that the captain's not your type…at all." He gave her his winning grin, the one that originally caught her interest.

"I can't believe the cops found stuff in my house that belonged to him. Pipe tobacco? I mean, c'mon, you know how I hate the smell of tobacco. And his stinky underpants in my laundry hamper? That's just too gross to even think about." She shuddered. "I've been set up, that's the only thing I can think of. But who set me up? And why?"

"I have no idea, Yo. None."

"How did someone get into my place? I never saw or heard anything. My garage is separate, and they found money in my glove compartment. Who'd sneak in and plant money in my car? Geez, I could lose my house, the yummery. If someone can frame me for murder then they could also kill me..."

Zac stood closer to her. "Yo, please try not to worry about it. I know it's not going to help if I tell you this, but I care about you, and I only want the best for you. Just know that I'm gonna help any way I can, and your parents will help, and you got a lot of people on your side."

He patted her on the shoulder and left the yummery. For a few seconds she watched him leave. Now that was the nice, caring Zac. A Zac that didn't even mention golf. She hadn't remembered him being that way.

A glance at the cupcake clock above the door showed just thirty minutes until closing. Although she planned to stay late and bake some more, part of her wanted to just go home and sleep as long as she could.

She went into the kitchen and saw BB dipping lemon frosted cupcakes in a bowl of toasted shredded coconut. "Hey BB, why don't you leave for the day, and I'll make sure you're clocked out at six. And can you work the six-to-six tomorrow or do you ...?"

"Oh, that's fine, I'll stay till six tonight, Yolanda."

"Now BB, I see you're almost done anyway, and I'll be happy to pay you for all your work. Really." She smiled, and the girl reluctantly coated the last cupcake. "I'll see you tomorrow at six?"

BB smiled. "Of course you will. And thanks so much, Yolanda. You're the best boss ever."

"I seriously doubt that, but thanks for saying that BB." Yolanda smiled and walked to the back of the shop and began pushing chairs under the tables.

"Well, good evening, pretty lady!" Mike O'Neill said as soon as he spotted her.

She stopped what she was doing, looked up and smiled. "Hello and welcome to Yolanda's Yummery." There was a pause as she studied the tall handsome Texan in a toned-down outfit of a light blue denim shirt and faded jeans. Only the silver and turquoise bolo tie hinted at the Lone Star State's origins. "Would you like a sample of our lemon and coconut cookies or cupcakes?"

He grinned. "Why that sounds delightful, miss."

She went over to the counter and lifted the lid to the sample tray. It shook in her hand and was on the verge of falling when Mike grabbed it from her and gently set it back down.

"Miss Yolanda, why you do look fit to be tied," Mike said. "I'm aware of your predicament. I saw it on the news, and it just doesn't make a lick of sense to me."

She nodded, trying not to show her sudden welling of tears. "It's been quite a day..."

"Yes ma'am, I imagine it has. And I think we can make it a whole lot better."

Yolanda wiped a hand across her eyes and when she was finished, looked up at his kindly amber eyes. "Oh? How would...?"

"I might suggest going for a ride in my new car for starters. And I have a little house on the beach. And maybe I can have my personal chef cook up a Texas-style barbeque. Or a Maine lobster? Or a...whatever you'd like Miss Yolanda."

"Are you serious?"

"Yes ma'am."

She grinned. "I can't say no. Let me get changed and tell my mom." She dashed off to the kitchen.

* * *

After a quick explanation to Abby, her mother smiled and was introduced to Mike. She stood in the back of the yummery plying him with samples and gave him a lemon coconut energy bar. Meanwhile, Yolanda was in the break room changing into a turquoise blouse and white jeans and matching sandals. A colorful daisy print cloth handbag dangled from her arm.

Yolanda removed her ponytail holder and put it in her purse. Whipping out a hairbrush, she brushed her long hair and returned the brush, exchanging it for a pair of sunglasses. When she stepped out, Mike gave a low whistle, and the twosome quickly left the store.

Just as they walked into the parking lot, Yolanda turned and looked up at the man. "My head's about to explode. I really need to go somewhere else. Thanks for stopping by and rescuing me!"

"The pleasure's all mine." He pulled his key fob out of his jeans pocket and flicked a switch. A loud double beeping noise emanated from a vehicle at the edge of the lot. It was a vehicle unlike any she had seen before.

Aside from the fact that the low-slung sports car was polished into a mirror like gloss, the two-tone red and black mode of transportation had attracted a cluster of admirers. "Even in Brentwood you don't see Bugattis every day," said a man in a beige business suit holding a laptop case.

An older man nodded. "My ex-wife's uncle had a used one. Even that cost about a mill..."

Two teenage boys gazed at the pristine Italian automobile.

"I want one of these when I get my license," one of them said. His friend burst out laughing.

Mike walked over to his car and gallantly opened the passenger's side door for Yolanda. "Please step inside," he said, smiling down at her and then glancing up to observe the gathering of admirers. He closed the door and went around the back of the Bugatti Veyron to let himself inside.

"Excuse me, what year is this car?" asked the man with the laptop.

"This year's model," Mike said, getting in and shutting the door.

"Wow must be nice," the man said. No one said anything because the next sound was that of the thunderous engine roaring to life. If Yolanda thought Zac's BMW M3 was loud, the Bugatti's 1,200 horsepower, 16-cylinder engine's reverberation was overwhelming. It was almost the same as a Formula 1's engine.

The spectators watched as the flashy car backed out and sped toward the mini mall's exit.

Yolanda squelched the urge to wave at them. She settled back into the kidskin soft leather interior smelling of newness and wealth. It was different from any other car she'd ever been inside. If she thought her new car had better pickup than her old car, what she felt when the Bugatti accelerated was closer to an airplane on takeoff.

"You gotta be careful handling this car," Mike said, speeding down a side street. "People who've never driven one can spin out when they first accelerate. This puppy goes from zero to 60 miles per hour in 2.46 seconds."

"That's super-fast! But I think that's a little above the speed limit around here." They laughed loudly and she looked out the tinted glass window as they approached Santa Monica

Boulevard heading west. In front of a café, several sidewalk diners watched the car whiz past.

Mike smiled. "It's fun seeing people's reactions. But hoo boy, the insurance is astronomical on this baby. And it's a real gas guzzler -- I only get about nine miles per gallon. That's why I'm glad I've also got a Ford F-150." He chuckled. "We can let this puppy ride on the PCH but for now I gotta keep it just under the speed limit. That way I won't hit any red lights."

Yolanda nodded. "Good idea. This is really a great car." She couldn't help noticing all the pedestrians noticing the Bugatti. People in other vehicles pointed and stared.

They hit the first red light at the crosswalk at the Third Street Promenade. On a hot June night, crowds of pedestrians were crossing Santa Monica Boulevard. Yolanda was enjoying the attention paid to the car and not her and smiled as everyone stared. Pointed fingers, longing glances, comments to others admiring the supercar. It was a surreal experience for someone who'd only driven economy cars.

She spotted someone familiar -- Nigel Garvey! He wore the same navy tracksuit and running shoes as he had that morning. Walking just behind and to his left was a petite young woman with short blonde hair and multiple earrings glittered in her ears. Oblivious to the vehicle, she was staring up at Nigel, talking to him as the man suddenly stopped in the middle of the street and gazed at the Bugatti. Directly at the passenger in the foreign sports car. And she stared back at him. She was surprised that he recognized her with her hair down and wearing sunglasses. *I should've worn a baseball cap*, she thought.

But there he was, walking closely with the woman Jeannie had described a few days ago. She knew that her employee was honest, but she had hoped Jeannie was wrong. Mike wasn't paying attention to the tea baron and his lady friend crossing his path. He was simply enjoying the show of awestruck car enthusiasts. His smile was as bright as it was the instant that engine revved to life.

Nigel and the woman walked away, and the light changed. She saw him with another woman, and he saw her in the passenger seat of an Italian supercar with another man.

* * *

Abby and Frederick were alone in the yummery. Yolanda had spoken to her father about being in Malibu for the next few hours. She explained about the storage lockers the captain had, what they contained, and that Tank and Chopper were trying to solve the case. "What the heck is detective Churchill doing? I thought this was his case?" Frederick asked.

"Your guess is as good as mine, dear." Abby sighed and munched on a double chocolate chip cookie. A pink yummy pack was open, the ribbon sitting on the counter. She stared into space and so did Frederick, when there was a loud knocking on the front door. Teagan stood there flanked by two large men.

"That must be Tank and Chopper," Abby remarked.

"How do you tell 'em apart?" Frederick wondered aloud.

They walked toward the front door. "I'm sure Teagan will let us know, dear."

Teagan entered the yummery first, followed by the tattooed Chopper who smiled and shook Frederick's hand. "Hey man, I love your work. I bought the limited-edition cake pedestal stand in misty mint green for my glass collection. It's like the centerpiece in my dining room."

Frederick grinned. "Thanks, I'm glad you like it. I might bring back an updated version in the near future...uh, are you Tank or Chopper?"

Teagan blushed and shrugged her shoulders. "Oops, my

bad. Frederick, this is Chopper, and I think he knows who you are. And this is Tank," she gestured toward the black-clad Italian who stepped forward and shook hands. "Where's Yolanda?"

"Well, she opted for a change of scenery," Abby said. "I encouraged her. If she's charged with murder she'll lose everything she's worked so hard for. And I don't think she'd be happy baking in prison."

"I can't see Yolanda baking in prison," Teagan said.

Tank looked around the yummery. "Well, she does have stripes on the walls..."

Chopper frowned. "That's insensitive, Tank."

"Just kidding, man." Tank said. "Okay, here's what's happening. Someone's gathering all the captain's movie memorabilia up and wants to sell it. But we don't know where it'll be sold yet. Most likely, it'll be through a private dealer. What I wanna do is see some private dealers and learn if any of them have been offered a whole buncha valuable stuff. Stuff that'll sell on the black market or overseas."

"Would you like some cookies before we go?" Abby asked.

Tank and Chopper smiled, unlike Teagan who held her belly.

"That's a great offer," Tank said and accepted the yellow yummy stacks that were presented to him and his friend.

"Thanks loads," Chopper said as he immediately opened the cellophane bag.

"I know you're watching your figure, Teagan," Abby said. "Okay, so are we all going in your car?"

"Whose car?" Tank asked.

"I don't know, that's why I'm asking. We're doing what we can to help Yolanda."

"Well, we drove over here in my car, so I was planning to

take that but what the heck do you folks know about private investigation techniques?"

"We've seen *Law and Order* and *Magnum P.I.* and *The Rockford Files*. You'll find us to be quick learners," Frederick stated. "Just because I blow glass and my wife makes batik art and teaches Pilates doesn't mean we..."

"Okay, fine, there's room for you. Follow us," Tank said. "But I'm driving."

"I'm riding in the back," Teagan said as she followed the group out the front door.

When they were all seated in the early 1970s vehicle, Tank called out, "Buckle up—it's the law." He flicked on the engine and backed out of the space, heading towards Grove Street. "I'm not taking the freeway—now I take surface streets between here and Hollyweird," he said, glancing into his rearview mirror. "Time for some tunes." Tank flicked on his DVD player and smiled when the lively sound of the saxophone of Sonny Rollins's "St. Thomas" filtered through the modern speakers.

Mike and Yolanda sat on a comfortable overstuffed couch in his huge glass-fronted living room overlooking the ocean. Debussy's piano music filled the room from invisible ceiling speakers. The sliding door was open, and they heard the rhythmic crashing of waves along the shoreline on the moonlit night. In the brightly lit kitchen behind them, the sounds of knives chopping on a wooden surface and pulverizing courtesy of a food processor. The aroma of mesquite-flavored meat hitting the grill and the boiling of a lobster in a pot competed to entice the couple with the savory scents of their elegant dinner. On the deck sat a linen-covered table with a lamp in the center next to an orchid arrangement in a crystal vase. Ornate crystal goblets contained sparkling water and a plate of various citrus slices. A bell rang and the couple sat down with their perfect view of the ocean, almost alone – only one other glass-fronted house within two hundred yards of them and it was clear that no one was home.

Yolanda had removed her sandals, and her bare feet caressed the soft rug that had been set out for the occasion. Across from her sat the handsome young Texan, linen napkin in his lap, at ease with the assortment of fine silverware stretched out on either side of the antique Royal Limoges china bowls that contained identical mixed greens salads.

The private chef, a middle-aged man with a tall cap and an immaculate white jacket, stepped out. A younger man that had the same broad forehead and high cheekbones, followed him. Only he wore a forest green apron and carried a large black serving tray.

The chef cleared his throat and proudly clasped his hands to his chest.

"Good evening Miss Yolanda and Mike. I have for you two of my specialties: Wagyu Kobe Filet Mignon, grilled to medium-rare perfection, and smothered in truffles and a side of arugula and curly kale. For the lovely lady, a freshly flown in Maine rock tail lobster. It's accentuated with a garlic butter herb sauce that is a secret New England recipe my own grandmother concocted." The chef stepped aside. The younger man smoothly set each dish in front of the couple.

"I hope you like the lobster, Yolanda." The chef and his assistant grinned.

"Thank you so much, it smells wonderful!" she said.

Mike was just as complimentary and a few seconds later, the two men bowed and hurried away, allowing the couple to be alone on the deck to enjoy their romantic dinner overlooking the ocean.

* * *

Around Wilshire and Spalding, the Buick's pace picked up. At the stoplight, Tank propped his long arm across the back of the seat and turned around to get a closer look. He nodded; it was the same white sedan that was following them ever since they left the yummery's parking lot.

"Okay, folks, we're being followed. Don't know if it's the cops or the media, and I don't wanna know. I just wanna put some distance between us and them."

He stepped on the accelerator and the car swerved left; Teagan's head almost hit the closed window. The car drove faster and faster and switched over to another street heading east, blasting through stoplights. A rundown van with no headlight ts almost ran into them. In the backseat, the three passengers held hands as the car sped down the side streets on the way to Hollywood.

The car slowed down and rounded a corner. Frederick glanced up and saw the lit Hollywood sign to his left. Tank slowed it even further as he navigated a pothole-filled alley. Finally, the Buick stopped and parked next to a dumpster. The headlights picked out the name of the establishment: Hollywood Yesteryear Memorabilia.

"Frederick, I'm going in there and I need you to act like a collector. Think you can do that?" asked Tank.

"I sure can," Frederick replied.

"Okay, good. I'm counting on you. Let's go around the side but I'll check on Fountainview Avenue just to make sure."

The men made their way over to the front of the small shop that looked deserted. Iron bars covered a window that displayed some old hardcover movie books. A faded red velvet backdrop prevented the inside of the store from being seen. The door had a tiny window covered by a curtain. An old-fashioned plastic

OPEN sign made sure no one saw inside the place. An arrow pointed to the doorbell. Tank rang it, and they heard the buzzing noise resounding throughout the store.

Light footsteps were heard. "We're closing in fifteen minutes," said the unfriendly voice of an older woman.

"That's fine, madam," Tank replied as the curtain parted a fraction of an inch and the door slowly creaked open.

The men walked into the musty shop that was dedicated to the golden years of Hollywood. Many of the items were displayed behind locked glass cases. Leather-bound and clothbound books, screenplays both bound and unbound. VHS and Beta tapes, some in original cardboard cases, metal film cans of various sizes and an array of colors glinting in the overhead lights. Movie posters adorned the walls, most were sun-faded with ripped edges. Others were stored in racks.

The proprietor sported frizzy white shoulder length hair and hunched over in her years-out-of-date cable knit sweater and skirt. On her chest was a red and white nametag: Olivia. She noticed Tank's gawking expression.

"I'm cold blooded, you nitwit. Now what do you fellas want?"

"Yes madam, my *nonna's* the same way. My name's Salvatore Ferrara. I want to know about people trying to sell off large amounts of expensive vintage TV and movie memorabilia?"

Olivia gave him an appraising look. "Oh, yeah, I know of your family." She glanced at the dusty bookshelf to her right. "Today, in fact. A young woman came in and offered what she said was an entire truckload of very valuable old Hollywood collectibles."

Frederick was thumbing through a 1953 issue of *Movie World Times*. "Who are you?" the woman asked.

"My name's Fred, I'm a friend of Ta...Salvatore's. I love old movie magazines."

"Well that one's ten bucks and it's not for sale unless you buy the whole year, and that rag came out twice a month so..."

Frederick gently replaced the issue. "Maybe I need to check with the wife. She's always getting on me about collecting..."

"Look, what else do you know about this woman who was here today?"

"Snippy. Very snippy attitude," the woman sniffed. "But she said she'd send her guys here tonight after we closed. Or should I say one hour after we closed. Means they'll be here at ten. And I hope to hell they're punctual because I don't want to miss *America's Talent Show* even though my neighbor made sure to record it for me but this way I can skip the damn commercials."

Tank gave her a huge grin. "My grandmother's favorite show also. Thank you so much for your help, we'll wait for them outside."

"But I said nothing..."

"Right. You said nothing."

Tank and Frederick returned to the Buick, which he moved a few yards away, so they had room to watch and wait for the arrival of the moving van. The five of them listened to John Coltrane's "Lush Life" for the next hour.

Mike and Yolanda had finished their meal. They shared some wine and an imported selection of European cheeses. The fruit consisted of kiwis and seedless green grapes. The bottle of red wine on the table was some sort of rare French vintage dating back to 1920. It was older than the money that the O'Neill family had earned when they first moved to Texas and began oil drilling and cattle ranching after World War I.

"Honey, you should drink more wine," Mike said, noting she'd barely consumed a quarter of her wine glass."

"Thanks, but a little of this goes a long way. Especially as it's such fine wine."

"The only kind for such fine company," he said, smiling broadly. "And heck, it only cost me $11,000 for this bottle. Not to brag, but some of the other ones I have are triple that amount."

"That much?" She'd heard of pricy wine before, just not in that league. The stuff didn't smell and taste as good as what was in her grandparents' breakfront cabinet. Root beer was much better – too bad she didn't insist on having that, although it didn't go too well with cheese and fruit.

While the full moon shone down on exclusive Broad Beach, she found herself wondering what Nigel was doing. And what about her parents? And Teagan? What were they going through right now as they tracked down the mysterious memorabilia that was being collected from all the storage lockers?

Ten o'clock came and went with no sign of any moving van. Ten past, ten-fifteen, and finally at twenty past the hour, a large Summerfield Moving Company van pulled up at the edge of the alley. A pair of thickset men in green uniforms emerged from the van and walked over to the back door of the memorabilia shop. One of them knocked, using three loud quick raps followed by two slower ones. They waited for several minutes until the old woman shuffled over and unlocked the door, slowly pushing it open.

Abby kept looking around, and finally she climbed over Teagan and opened the door. It squeaked, startling the movers, and two gunshots were fired. Abby fell out of the car, landing in the middle of the alley. Frederick and Teagan were frozen in disbelief as they stared at her motionless body. The moving men raced back to their van. The shop's back door slammed shut.

In the front seat, Tank and Chopper removed their guns and crawled out of the car, passenger side first. "We can't leave her here," Tank said. Chopper grunted in affirmation, ducking lower and looking around him.

The moving van's engine revved up and it backed out of the alley. Tank and Chopper ran down the alley, holding their guns in front of them, pursuing the moving van that was thrown in reverse, and the tires squealed as it made its way back to Fountainview.

Abby suddenly sat up and Tank and Chopper rushed over to her side. She shook her head. "What happened? What's going on?"

Frederick and Teagan scrambled out of the car and went over to the distraught woman, helping her to her feet. "It's okay, dear," Frederick said. "You'll be fine. We'll be staying with Yolanda tonight."

She nodded as they went back to the car, and she collapsed into the back seat.

Tank did a once around the car and breathed a sigh of relief. "We're really lucky, no one got hit and the Electra Lady wasn't even touched."

* * *

Yolanda felt the gentle sea breeze ruffle her hair. She gazed at Mike and felt a sense of peace and calmness that she hadn't experienced since the whole fiasco began last week. How unlike her chaotic weekend, of first being questioned by the detective at the police station, and worse, her cottage being searched. Now the events seemed less painful and more distant. Mike reached over, touched her hand, and then held it. Warmth and waves of radiant energy flowed between them. Each second they touched made her happier and happier and she wanted to get closer to him. He grasped her hand a little tighter and she didn't protest. The breeze grew lighter, and her temperature grew warmer in the late evening.

"Hey sugar, wanna see my bedroom?"

Yolanda's eyes widened when she heard that tacky question. The warmth vanished. She pulled her hand away. "No thanks, not tonight." She looked at her watch and stood up. "But I've got to get back home and feed my cats...can you please drive me back to the yummery? My car's still there."

Mike sat there and blinked a few times. "You sure can put a damper on a fine date, Miss Yolanda."

She shook her head. "No, you just tried to go too far too fast. I'm a good girl."

* * *

Yolanda finally drove into her driveway only to see her parents' car pulled to the side and the kitchen light on. She parked in the garage, and when she got out, it was dark. A loud thumping noise was heard in the far-right hand corner. She rushed to the light switch on the left wall and snapped on the light. Looking around, she saw nothing and tentatively walked over to the area stacked with boxes where she'd heard the sound. There was no noise. The boxes were untouched. Once outside the garage, she double-checked the side door to make sure it was locked. The feeling of being watched was very strong. The security light above the garage was on and as she walked to the foot of the driveway, Yolanda looked up and down the street. No one was walking around the area. No traffic drove in either direction. The only vehicles she saw were those parked along Willowbrook and Dove. Who was watching her? The police? The media? The person who had kidnapped or killed the captain? Quickly, she turned around and went inside, quietly shutting the door behind her. The food and water bowls were half-full, and she looked in the living room and saw the cats on the couch sound asleep, Ms. Chef curled up against Mr. Whisker.

Yolanda made sure the kitchen door was locked, and then removed her shoes. She silently walked into the living room and checked the windows. None were unlocked. The front door was locked. The feeling didn't disappear. Uneasily, she tiptoed down the hallway. The guest room door was shut, and the light was off. Her father's snores were all she heard.

CHAPTER 9

WEDNESDAY

Well before sunrise, Yolanda awoke and knew that by five-thirty she needed to be at the yummery to open for the carpenters. BB would arrive by six. More baking would be done throughout the day, and she hoped that the new system would be more efficient for everyone. It would also allow her to get extra sleep.

She thought about her date with the Texan and wished she could have discussed it with her mother. Mom always stressed the importance of not being "too eager" on the first date. Or the second. And it didn't matter if you dined at a fast-food restaurant or a place with Michelin Stars or a millionaire's Malibu Beach house ... rushing into an intimate relationship wasn't the way to go.

Yolanda unlocked her car and flung her purse into the back seat. It was still dark, and her headlights flicked on with the ignition and lit up the front of the garage. She tapped the genie to open the door and backed out, pausing to hit the remote again to shut the door. She backed the car out, neither speeding nor going at granny pace. There was rarely any predawn traffic on her street. Backing onto Willowbrook, she turned the steering wheel sharply and when she backed onto the street, her car about to travel south, an oncoming beige sedan sped towards her vehicle. The bright headlights grew closer, the engine and speeding noises the tires made were headed right at the Honda and she instinctively swerved towards the house, barely missing the fence. The car roared past her, and the crunching sound of the back left-hand section scared her. She looked up and to the left. The sedan drove beneath a streetlight and for an instant; she saw a silhouette of the driver. It was the slight figure of a woman with a ponytail.

The noise of the hit and run caused lights to snap on in nearby houses. She shakily reached inside her car, found her purse on the floor, and reached in to find her cell phone. Grabbing it, she dialed 911 and then looked up to see her parents rushing out of her house wearing their bathrobes over pajamas. "Yolanda are you okay?" Abby went over and hugged her daughter.

Frederick looked at the car and saw thick scrape marks along the backside of it, but nothing was broken, and the tire hadn't been hit. "Sure are some bad drivers out here," he said.

"Look, you need to go back to sleep. I'll take care of this, mom and dad."

Her parents hesitated and she insisted. "I'll wait here till the police show up. I'm fine, my car has minor scrapes but it's drivable. Really, it'll be okay..."

Reluctantly they turned around and went back into the house.

Twenty minutes later, a police cruiser showed up, the uniformed officer getting out and looking at the minor damage. His nametag read Wallace and the stout man wasn't much of a smiler. He brusquely asked Yolanda for her identification, insurance, and car registration. Upon seeing her name, he glared at her. "I know you may be a murder suspect."

"Look, officer, someone tried to run into me when I backed

out of my own driveway. It happened so fast. I was on my way to work and a car with bright headlights came at me. I think they wanted to kill me."

He quickly jotted down the notes in his notepad. "Who wants to kill you?"

"That's what I really want to know," Yolanda said. "All I saw was a woman with a ponytail in the car. It was right underneath the streetlight."

* * *

Her workday was busy from the moment she arrived twenty minutes late. The carpenters along with Jeannie and BB were waiting outside the yummery, all looking worried until she arrived. The weather was warm but overcast and there was a chance of rain.

Instead of a cloudburst of water, Detective Churchill showed up with the mandatory order to visit the nearby police station to participate in a lineup. He would need to see her at two o'clock. *Oh, yay rah a police lineup—definitely on my top ten list of things I need to do today*, she thought angrily.

"I'll be there at two," she informed the detective. "But I need to call my lawyer first."

The detective quickly left Yolanda's office. She watched him depart and noticed he wore a dark suit, and his shoulders were slumped. The man sure could use an energy bar. "Detective, wait a second!" She got up and went over to the baking rack that he had just passed. She grabbed a wax tissue from the table, pulled a lemon coconut energy bar off the rack, and handed it to the man. "Here, looks like you could use this."

For an instant, he hesitated, and then a smile appeared. "Yeah, I skipped breakfast this morning." He took a bite and shook his head. "I love lemon – it's tangy."

She giggled. "Yes it is. I think it's a descriptive word."

"Thanks Yolanda. I appreciate this. I also appreciate your cooperation."

"Absolutely. I want you to find whoever did this. This morning a car drove down my street and tried to run me off the road."

He nodded. "I read it in the report. Sorry to hear about that. Looks like no one else saw it. Too bad there wasn't any video footage or any witnesses."

That afternoon she met Kyle Newman at the police station and his eyes lit up when he saw the large pink canvas tote bag she carried. "Hey Yolanda, great to see you." He looked down at the bag, noticing it was filled with a variety of baked goodies. "Good idea to bring samples," he said. Got any doughnuts?"

"Nope. I don't make doughnuts. But I have cookies, brownies and a variety of energy bars."

Officer Aikens walked by and gave her a huge smile. "Yolanda how good to see you again! I was wondering if you had any oatmeal raisin cookies by any chance?"

"As a matter of fact, I do." She reached into the bag, pulled out one of her popular yummy 6-pack cookie stacks, and handed it to him.

"Awesome! Thanks so much, Yolanda!"

Kyle watched the transaction. "You do the best p.r. for your business. Now let me explain what happens. You'll be spending just a few minutes lining up with some other people. All you do is stand there. A resident of the marina called and reported seeing a woman showing up at the captain's yacht a few times since the beginning of May. She says the woman had bags of fast food with her."

Yolanda nodded. "Okay. So, um, I just stand there, and she can see me, but I can't see the resident?"

"Correct."

Detective Churchill approached them from the hallway. "Good afternoon Ms. Carter, Mr. Newman. Please follow me."

"Okay." She followed him, and they walked in the first door on the right.

It was a small room with a large, tinted glass window in front of a table and three chairs. "Okay, Yolanda, just go through that door on the right and we'll call the other women in so you can all line up and we'll call out directions to you on the intercom. Otherwise, you won't be able to hear what we're saying in here."

She left the room, stepping over to the wall, which had a height chart. She stood in front of that, put her hand over her head, and stepped away to note the height.

"Yolanda, what are you doing?"

She heard Churchill's voice but didn't see him, only her mirrored image. "I'm seeing how tall I am. I forget if I'm five seven or five eight."

"Go back to the wall and stand straight," said Kyle. There was a pause. "Okay, it looks like you're five seven and a half."

"No, it looks closer to five seven," Detective Churchill remarked.

One of the side doors opened and four women in their mid-twenties to late- thirties entered. Three were gangly with dark hair and the youngest was a petite red head wearing shorts and a tank top.

A police officer escorted in the elderly witness. Slightly built with a jet-black pageboy showing white at the roots, she eagerly walked up to the window. She adjusted her glasses and peered about an inch away from the window. Suddenly she chuckled and tapped on the glass with her twisted knuckles. "You have a celebrity in there!" exclaimed Mrs. Adams.

The detective and lawyer exchanged glances. "We do?" asked the detective.

Mrs. Adams nodded. "Indeed, you do. I saw this young lady on TV being interviewed and went to her bakery and my oh my--those brownies are the best." She smiled. "Yoo hoo, sweetheart, you have a great little bakery." She tapped on the window.

Detective Churchill winced. "I'm afraid she can't hear you, Mrs. Adams."

The woman turned around and suddenly noticed the pink canvas tote bag sitting on the table. "That's the place, Yolanda's Yummery!" She rubbed her hands together as she walked over and looked at the bag, about to reach for it.

Kyle stood there watching the scene and said nothing. It was up to the detective to defuse the situation. "Mrs. Adams are you sure that you didn't see Yolanda on the captain's yacht. Either with or without Captain Angus Prescott?"

The woman froze and reluctantly stopped looking at the bag of goodies. She focused on Churchill. "Sir, I would recognize the suspect and I can assure you that Yolanda wouldn't be hanging around with the likes of that man."

"Okay, thank you very much. Did you see the other women in the lineup?" asked Churchill.

She shook her head. "I'll take another look, but I don't think so." She went back to the window and peered out the glass and shook her head. "No, not any of them." She stepped back to the table. "Can I have one of those cookie bags do you think? Do you know how much they cost?"

"You'll have to ask Yolanda. I'll get her." Churchill switched on the intercom and spoke into it. "Thank you for your time, ladies. Please exit to your right. Yolanda Carter, please return to the viewing room." He clicked off the intercom.

Yolanda looked around, wide-eyed, and then went over to the other door and went inside the small room. Mrs. Adams saw her and waved. "I really love your brownies and I want you to know my daughter served your magical love cakes at one of her afternoon teas and it was such a lovely occasion. Now, how much for one of your cookie bags?"

"Oh, it's free today. Please help yourself."

"Are you sure? That's so kind of you!" The woman reached into the tote bag and pulled out a yellow stack of lemon coconut cookies. She tried opening it, but the slippery cellophane bag slipped and fell to the table.

Detective Churchill stepped over to her side. "Ma'am, let me get that for you." He untied the ribbon and extended the little bag to her.

She smiled at the detective. "Thank you very much, youngster." She reached in and took one out, sniffing it. "Oh my, I love anything lemony!" Mrs. Adams took a bite of the cookie and chewed it slowly, making a loud smacking sound. "Oh, my word, this is beyond good!"

"Thanks, Mrs. Adams, so glad you like it. I'm a big fan of lemon coconut myself," Yolanda said.

"Oh my, where are my manners!" Mrs. Adams exclaimed, extending the package. "Here you are gentlemen, please help yourselves."

"Don't mind if I do," Kyle said, taking one and plopping the whole cookie in his mouth. He tilted his head to the side and closed his eyes. "Not bad, not bad at all. Very lively flavor. Please try one, Churchill."

"No thanks, I had a lemon coconut energy bar – and it's nice. I wasn't overloaded with energy but at the same time I don't have the afternoon sugar craving like I usually get around this time." He glanced at the clock on the wall.

"Thank you for coming in here today Mrs. Adams and Ms. Carter. It's appreciated." He smiled and walked over to the door to open it. Yolanda went over to the table and picked up her bag.

No one in that room was expecting the crowd of police officers, detectives and police employees that gathered right outside the doorway, many of them looking at the tote bag that Yolanda was carrying.

* * *

Yolanda returned to her shop along with the afternoon rush. Nick had set up a new tips jar saying:

TIPPING MAKES THE WORLD A SWEETER PLACE!

Several office workers were crowding into the yummery for their sugary snacks. A mother and three preschool aged children with chocolate-smeared faces had their hands on the glass as they watched Nick removing the brownies from the tray and boxing them up. Three couples sat at tables and feasted on cupcakes and cookies. Next door, the application of the wallpaper and painting were nearing completion. Yolanda inspected it, carefully moving among the tarps and paint cans. She returned to the yummery and set out a tray of brownies, making a note to clean the glass as soon as she finished.

Lydia was coming from the back of the store holding two plastic bottles of milk and she went up to the counter to pick up a decadent chocolate Magical Cake of Love. As she handed her credit card to Nick, her cell phone rang. She pulled out a red be-jeweled-cased phone and answered it. "What?" she said abruptly as she paused to listen to the caller. "Yeah, I know. I can be there by then."

Yolanda straightened up and cocked her head to one side, listening intently when she overheard the voice. She clutched the tray in front of her and slowly turned to her right to see where the voice was originating. Seeing Lydia, a twice-daily appreciated guest, she slipped into the background near the edge of the cash wrap area and watched as the woman lifted the tote bag with the cake and beverages and left the yummery. The woman in the severe navy suit quickly went past her on the sidewalk and breezed by Detective Churchill's unmarked car a few spaces down. Yolanda put down her tray, removed the window cleaner and cloth and walked around the counter, but another appreciated guest stood there so she couldn't get involved in a cleaning task. She went to the window to wipe the front door and saw Lydia's progress as she headed across the parking lot towards San Vicente.

Is she the killer? Will the detective believe me if I tell him? What about me saying I'd been on the captain's yacht looking for evidence? Yolanda thought, watching the woman walking away from her line of sight.

A Channel 20 news van drove up to the edge of the lot and Yolanda swiped the fingerprints off the main section of the front door. She stepped back as though admiring her cleaning job, then looked up at the clock. Grabbing the bottle and rag, she went back to her office and sat down, picking up the phone. A minute later and she said, "Teagan, can you and Tank and Chopper come over here please..."

Soon after the yummery closed for the evening, Detective Churchill's car drove out of the parking lot. A black unmarked sedan took its place. Tank's Buick was parked at the other end of the lot and he, Teagan and Chopper got out of the vehicle and headed over to the yummery. Once inside, the four of them went back to the kitchen. "Okay, everyone, I want to let you know what's going on...I think I may have found the killer." Yolanda said.

CHAPTER 10

THURSDAY

Yolanda had gone home to sleep but all she did was clean the litter box and feed the cats. Still restless, she went into her bathroom and saw the package of bath products that Heather had sent over to test. Inside was a bright pink bubble bath cupcake that Heather was concocting for her winter collection. She smelled the awesome bath product, barely refraining from taking a bite of the strawberry and vanilla scented concoction. Smiling, she tossed it into the bathtub right beneath the running water. Immediately a fountain of foam filled the tub, and the aroma of sweet strawberries permeated the bathroom.

Removing her dirty clothing and leaving them on the floor in a pile, she stepped into the warm bathwater and slid beneath the abundance of fragrant bubbles. Sighing, Yolanda felt her muscles relaxing and the whirling thoughts in her head slowing down. She would happily sell the bubble bath cupcakes in her shop, and she knew that Heather Hathaway's Lotions & More had a new hit product. She flipped the faucet off with her foot, leaned against the back of the bathtub, and dozed off.

* * *

The lingering fragrance of strawberries underscored with a dash of vanilla comforted her as she pulled into the parking lot outside the yummery at five o'clock. The black car was still there, and the driver was asleep behind the wheel. She giggled upon seeing that and decided to offer him a cup of coffee and some cookies.

Moments before the yummery opened, a white Kia four-door rental car drove slowly into the parking lot and pulled into a spot near San Vicente. She saw that Tank and Chopper were inside and smiled, glad to see that the plan was unfolding. The next step would occur when the shop opened, and the appreciated guests arrived.

At opening time, the first person to rush inside was Lydia Sloan. She wore a beige pants suit, and her hair was loose, swept back with a wide headband. She wore no makeup and the circles beneath her eyes contrasted with her pale complexion.

"Excuse me, I need my usual fancy vanilla buttercream cupcake and a small coffee," Lydia said, moving over to the counter area near the cupcakes. Jeannie blinked a few times before answering calmly. "Yes, Lydia. One moment please."

The Goldbergs and some office workers arrived followed by a smiling guy wearing a backwards baseball cap, a faded shirt and loose-fitting sweatpants. "Morning Yolanda!" he called out. "Good to see ya!"

"Hello!" Yolanda said to the young man who moved over to the samples tray and helped himself to a chocolate chip cookie piece. He ran in place and did a couple of jumping jacks. "Hey, good cookie. Now, I got a joke for you...wanna hear it?"

"Sure, why not?" Yolanda watched the guy and at the same time she saw that Lydia was receiving her coffee and the bag containing the cupcake.

"Okay, get this...what do you call a dozen of Yolanda's Yummery brownies?"

Hilda Goldberg giggled. "That's easy – really good!"

The guy did a couple of jumping jacks. "Yeah, nice try. The answer is killer brownies!" He burst out laughing.

Lydia gave him a scowl as she quickly left the yummery. Yolanda watched her departing, paying little attention to the guy with the bad joke.

"Okay, so I get another one. What's Yolanda's next flavor of the week?"

Jeannie nodded. "I know – strawberry."

The guy was running in place and laughed. "No..." he began shadow boxing. "I'll tell you -- death by chocolate."

One of the younger office workers groaned. Yolanda rolled her eyes.

Al Goldberg went up to the springy young comedian. "Hey, I got one for you. Knock knock."

The comedian bounced around with his shadow boxing routine and did a side kick, almost hitting the circular rack. "Who's there?"

Al replied. "Go."

He stopped moving and stared at the senior citizen. "Go who?"

"Go find yourself a funny joke."

There was a chorus of laughter from the employees and most of the appreciated guests. The young guy smiled and turned around, did a quick salute, and left the yummery.

Yolanda walked over to Al and handed him a chocolate walnut brownie. "Here you go, Al. thanks for that!"

Al smiled as he accepted the rich protein-packed brownie. "One of your rich and decadent chocolate walnut brownies! Are you tryin' to kill me?"

There was more good-natured laughter, and his wife nudged his stomach with her elbow.

* * *

The white rental sedan was parked on a side street just off Wilshire Boulevard. Tank and Chopper watched as Lydia rushed into a twelve-story office building. "Tank, where did Yolanda say that she worked?"

"I think an accounting agency," Chopper said. "Let's go check it out."

The men got out of the car and went inside the expansive marble-floored lobby with a fountain and plants along either side. In front of the double elevator bank was a directory and both men scanned it. "Sixth floor. Bates and Hornsby, Certified Public Accountants," Tank said quietly.

"Right, now let's see what's the intel on Lydia Sloan." He looked at the uniformed balding man behind the centrally located information desk. "I'll bet a C note or two will get us what we need."

After a briefcase-toting man attached a visitor's badge to his suit jacket, Tank went over to the uniformed man and read his nametag aloud. "Good morning Mr. Holt, fine morning it is. I was wondering if you know anything about a Bates and Hornsby employee named Lydia Sloan?" He flicked his wrist and two crisp folded hundred-dollar bills showed up in his palm.

Mr. Holt gave a quick nod, flicked off a computer camera switch to his right, and accepted the cash gift. "Yes I do. How long has she worked there? What her hours are? Anything more specific?"

"Just her hours and what kind of car she drives, and does she park beneath this building?" Tank asked.

"Easy enough. She works from seven fifteen to five fifteen just about every weekday. I know that she has a silver Ford Explorer—I think it's only two or three years old. Has a roof rack. It's parked underneath on the west side of level B. Anything else?"

"That'll do it. Thanks, Mr. Holt."

"Glad to help." He smiled and quickly reached under the desk and pushed the button to activate the cameras as soon as the men hit the front door.

* * *

Just before closing time, Tank and Chopper stopped off at the yummery and bought several brownies and cupcakes. They also wanted the yummy 6-pack cookie stacks in assorted flavors. "Can I meet with you in your office?" Tank asked Yolanda.

She closed the door and sat behind her desk, knowing what he was about to tell her was confidential. He slipped her a piece of paper.

"I'd suggest memorizing the address and throwing it out. As you can see, Lydia lives about a mile or two from here. Me and Chopper are going over there early tomorrow morning -- before she leaves for work. Whatever you do, don't go over there. We'll take care of this." He stood up to go. "Have any questions?"

"Yes I do. But they'll be answered tomorrow."

He grinned. "Good. That's what I wanna hear. Good night, Yo."

"Good night Tank."

After closing the shop and watching BB and Nick leaving, she returned to her office. The slip of paper was still on her desk. She looked at it and shoved it in her jeans' front pocket. She picked up the phone and called Teagan. The call went to voicemail.

"Teagan, I have Lydia's address. Meet me there at eight if you can. It's the Harper-Palms Building on 866 Harper Lane, unit 26. The cross street is Wendell Avenue."

Yolanda sat behind her desk and pulled out her Beverage Bar file to check up on the work status. A half hour later she heard loud banging on the front door. She closed the file and got up, rushing into the yummery. Teagan was at the front door. Yolanda unlocked it and let her friend inside.

"Hey, Yo, I got your message. I used to know someone that lived there. He was really hot, but he worked in retail and had to get a roommate to live there 'cause he never made enough money." She shook her head. "I forgot his name...hey, are you sure you want to go there and..."

Yolanda nodded. "I have to make sure about this. I have to see for myself. I don't blame you if you don't come with me. It's my mess, not yours. For some reason that woman hates me enough to set me up for murder, and I know she hit my car deliberaately...but I can't figure it out. Why would she be trying to ruin my life?"

"Yo, you know the world is full of crazy people. And this city really has its fair share of them," Teagan said.

"Yeah, tell me about it. So, I'm going to drive over there."

"Okay, that means I'm riding shotgun," Teagan said.

"You're my BFF for sure," Yolanda said and smiled. "I owe you big time for this."

"Don't forget -- I have a very good memory." Teagan giggled.

"You mean a very good selective memory," Yolanda teased her friend as they stepped out of the yummery.

The brick two-story Harper-Palms apartment building was as plain and unassuming as the others in the area. On both sides of the street were bumper-to-bumper parked cars and Yolanda had to park on the far side of Wendell Avenue.

They returned to the building and noted the wrought iron locked security gate behind the wall of mailboxes. An older man in a plaid shirt and baggy shorts hurried out, almost bumping into Teagan who smiled winningly at him. "Pardon me, miss," he said as he stared at her tight-fitting black tank top and Yolanda grabbed the edge of the gate and slipped inside the courtyard area. Teagan followed her, and they headed for the outdoor staircase on the other side of the concrete courtyard.

Unit 26 was at the back of the two-story building and a small potted palm tree with more brown fronds than green ones sheltered them from view. Both young women paused for an instant before knocking. The only sound that emanated from the unit was that of low voices; either a TV was on, or else Lydia was talking to someone.

Yolanda stood in front of the door and hesitated. What if Lydia wasn't alone? What if that wasn't Lydia inside the apartment? What if she called Detective Churchill and told him she had located the suspect—the real suspect? She took a deep breath and loudly knocked on the door.

The noise inside stopped. There was the sound of approaching footsteps. Loud footsteps. Uh oh! Yolanda backed away slightly and Teagan almost bumped into her.

The door swung open and a muscular man with unruly dark hair blocked the entrance. He wasn't a tall man, and he wore a black tracksuit with a partially unzipped jacket. His skimpy mustache had crumbs in it and his cheeks were acne ridden. "What do you want?" He narrowed his eyes at Yolanda as he flexed his arms and chest to appear more intimidating.

"I want to know what's going on," Yolanda said as she pushed past him and walked into the living room. Teagan followed her friend and the two of them stood at the edge of the carpeted room with a large brown sofa upon which another man sat with his high-top sneakers resting on a coffee table. The TV was on, and he was watching a baseball game when the uninvited women distracted his attention. He stood up, almost spilling a can of beer. His resemblance to the first man was striking. He wore holy jeans and a black hoodie advertising a trendy men's clothing store.

"What the hell are you two...?"

Lydia rushed into the living room from the kitchen. She was holding a handgun, pointing it at Yolanda and Teagan. Still wearing her office attire, Lydia smirked at the women and looked at the mustachioed guy standing near the front door. Shifting the gun, it was pointed at the man.

"Richie, close the door now."

He kicked it shut with his foot.

"Richie, use your hands. This isn't like the barn you and Damian were raised in. Now you and Damian watch these two...intruders."

"We're intruders and you're what...a murderer?" Yolanda said. "These two dingbats couldn't keep us out. Now why the hell are you doing this to me?"

"I got you on trespassing and breaking and entering. I could shoot you and your friend and still be within my legal rights."

A loud crashing noise was heard from the back of the apartment. Everyone froze for an instant.

"Richie, go see if the cap..." Lydia didn't finish her sentence as she ran out of the room and down a hallway to her left.

Everyone rushed after her and reached the small bedroom, which Lydia stood inside, reflected by the mirrored closet door that covered one wall. Lying on the floor was a black track suited Captain Angus Prescott with his arms tied behind his back, his ankles bound with rope and his mouth sealed with duct tape. A soiled blue bandana was wrapped around his forehead and flecks of dried blood were noticeable. He looked up at the five younger people and squirmed on the brown textured carpeting like a fish thrown onto a dock.

"Mmmmfffff, mmmmfff," he said, wiggling desperately, trying to loosen the binding ropes.

"Shut up, old man!" Lydia shouted, pointing the gun at him. "I'm ready to pull the trigger and end it all!"

Richie and Damian shook their heads almost in unison. "Look, cuz, we can't kill him. We gotta keep him alive. He's worth more alive…"

"You shut up birdbrain. You were supposed to drop that stuff off at the memorabilia shop and you two ran like little girls."

"There was a dead woman in the alley. Well, me and Damian thought she was dead, so we left."

"I can't believe you two jerks are my cousins. You seem to get dumber every day." She waved her gun at them. "Now pick up the captain and put him back on the bed."

"You kidnapped him?" Yolanda asked.

"No doofus, I didn't. They did." She pointed her gun from her cousins back to Yolanda and Teagan.

The men carefully picked up the captain and returned him to the double bed shoved against the wall. He looked different minus his captain's duds; the black tracksuit was the same kind the cousins wore and featured the brand name in huge white letters. Unlike the cousins, the captain wore dirty socks.

"Okay, tie these girls up like you did the captain. We'll get rid of them all tomorrow. I'm formulating a plan."

They paused, staring at Lydia. "You wanna get rid of all of them?" Damian asked, looking nervously at Yolanda and Teagan.

"I thought you had decent hearing, Damian. Apparently not." She waved the gun in his direction. "Get movin' now!" she demanded.

"Okay, okay," he paused, running his fingers through his messy hair. "Dude, where's the rope?"

"I don't know," Richie said. "I thought you had it last."

"Nuh uh, I thought you did. I …"

"Idiots!" Lydia shouted. "Try looking in the utility drawer in the kitchen. The one next to the sink. It's where I always keep it!"

"Yes ma'am," Richie said, hurrying out of the bedroom.

Lydia glared at the women with narrowed eyes. "You think you're such a great baker," she said to Yolanda. "You think you're so wonderful, don't you?"

Yolanda stared uneasily at the woman holding the gun barely a foot away from her and decided to keep the answers minimal. "Um, not really."

Richie returned carrying a spool of rope. "Here it is."

Lydia nodded. "So, where's the scissors? Or utility knife? How will you cut it, with those nasty teeth of yours?"

"Oh." He turned to leave.

"Same drawer, doofus." She shook her head. "I swear, I have the stupidest cousins in the world. I'm still amazed they can tie their own shoelaces and drive a truck."

"I've got a knife," Richie said as he rushed back into the room.

Lydia saw the man holding up a slender butter knife. "No, idiot, I told you the utility drawer to the left of the sink, not the cutlery drawer which is to the right...do I have to do this myself?"

"No, I gotcha..." he raced out of the room and was back a minute later holding up a box cutter. "Will this work?"

"Yes, wonderful. Now tie them up and put them on the bed. They can keep the captain company."

Richie went up to Teagan and began wrapping the rope around her wrists. He cut off a long piece of rope and handed the spool to Damian who took care of securing Yolanda's wrists and ankles. A few minutes later they were sitting on the bed next to the captain, who'd fallen asleep.

Richie giggled as he looked at the three people on the bed. "He can have a threesome."

"No, a twosome, there's only two women." Damian smiled at Yolanda and Teagan.

"No, it's a threesome because there are three people on the bed," Richie said.

Damian shook his head. "You're wrong. Two women and one man is a … oh, I see. Um, yeah, I guess you're kinda right."

"I am right. I'm not kinda right."

"You're both pathetic. Heck, everyone in this room, except for me, is pathetic," Lydia complained.

"That's your opinion, lady." Teagan said.

Lydia stuck the gun up against Teagan's neck. "Want to repeat that?"

Teagan stared straight ahead, trying to ignore the accountant.

"Good, I didn't think so." Lydia pulled the gun away.

"Tell us why you're doing this," Yolanda said. "I really want to know. So does my friend."

"I'm sure you both do. Well, okay, I'll be nice and play fair. You should know why before tomorrow at sunrise. In fact, in twenty-four hours you won't be alive anymore and soon after that your yummery will go out of business." She laughed. "Don't look so shocked, Yolanda, I owe you an explanation. But I don't want you to think I'm a competitor. Well, not really." She paused, shifting her weight. "It all began when I walked into the West Pico Golf Shop in March and met Zac Field. Your ex-boyfriend…"

* * *

On a blustery March evening with an undelivered threat of rainfall and some ominous claps of thunder, Lydia Sloan walked into the pro shop to buy her boss a golf-themed birthday gift. Adding shirts to a clothes rack stood a tall man wearing golfing attire. He smiled and welcomed her into the shop, saying he was there to assist her if she needed anything, and she was all smiles herself; a novelty for the serious woman who would turn thirty-six next month. Working with numbers never made her smile unless they were the right ones. When she looked at the younger man, she knew he was the right equation to her mathematical question of when would she find love?

Although Lydia wasn't ever one of the "pretty ones, or the cute ones" like her mother had told her over the years, she was accommodating enough to capture Zac's interest. His former girlfriend of eight months had never even gone to second base with him. That's what he told her during their first night together in unit 26 of the Harper-Palms. She'd seen Yolanda interviewed on TV, the internet and in various local magazines and newspapers to know that she was genuinely beautiful and a "real sweetheart, a real nice girl," said Zac.

One afternoon when Lydia was at the yummery, she saw a former client from the Beverly Hills accounting firm where she had worked for five years. She remembered that disgusting Angus Prescott who dressed like a shipwrecked captain, owned a yacht and stored his expensive Hollywood memorabilia in various storage units. The man begged for money or scrounged through garbage cans. A decade ago, her firm estimated that his collection alone was worth three million dollars. His estate was valued at about twenty million, including the yacht and the mansion in Beverly Hills, which was still vacant. Yet the man was a walking, stinking embarrassment. All that money not being spent when it would help her out of her boring existence. There was plenty of money to renovate that mansion. Old Captain Angus Prescott could provide that luxurious lifestyle that Lydia had craved all her life.

From the time she was in middle school, Lydia worked. Her divorced mother made her clean the apartment in a low-income section of Riverside. The mother told her she wasn't pretty enough to date and have fun. And she laughed when her daughter didn't even make the first cut at cheerleader tryouts. The only solid advice the widowed Mrs. Sloan ever gave Lydia was to stay in school and get a business degree. She bounced around doing auditing and accounting until she was hired at the Beverly Hills accounting firm, but it went out of business when the owner died. Lydia's job at Bates and Hornsby, Certified Public Accountants didn't pay as well and some of her duties bordered on secretarial. Being older wasn't better even in the allegedly more stable world of accounting. Or was it that she wasn't aging as well, being in a loveless, boring existence prior to meeting Zac?

However, Zac was still in love with Yolanda. He talked about her baking, her cats, her house in the Valley, and even her parents. When questioned closely about his former girlfriend's habits, he revealed where she kept her spare key for the house and the garage, and about the many hours she worked to keep the yummery going.

On the eve of Lydia's birthday, she hatched the plan—attract the captain's interest and marry him. Luring him with brownies or Magical Cakes of Love would capture his heart – and his substantial assets. Even if she had to invite him back to her place like she did with Zac, it would be worth it. Sure, Zac was young and handsome but had less money than she did. The Biodome Mini Golf Course idea was only that—something Zac desperately wanted. He'd enthusiastically explained that the mini golf course would be encased in a biodome at the edge of Simi Valley. It would be unique. He wanted it to be open 24/7 and it didn't matter what the weather was like, the inside temperature would always be seventy degrees and it would always be perfect for mini golf. Lydia thought that if the concept worked and was successful, fine. But it wouldn't work overnight. Maybe she could marry the captain and finance the Biodome idea and then wind up with Zac.

* * *

"So, you liked Zac romantically? But you liked the captain for his money?" Yolanda asked.

"Of course. Zac's cute and has a good business idea. But the captain's loaded." Lydia replied.

Teagan nodded. "I didn't realize he was so rich until last week. I can understand being interested in his money."

"You were the one who planted the pipe and his underwear in my laundry hamper, right?"

Lydia smiled and waved the gun towards the window. "Right. I broke into your garage and planted the money in your car. When I went into your house to get your car keys you didn't even wake up. You're such a sound sleeper."

"Maybe she's a sound sleeper because she works like 100 hours a week," Teagan said.

"I worked hard all my life. Never was handed anything. I'm not a pretty girl. I can't have a lah de dah life like Yolanda. I can't win a lottery and open a yummery. When I play the lottery, I'm lucky if I hit one number. I can't be the good girl because I get to be the accommodating girl. Or the other woman. Things aren't easy for me. I've never been the best...like what the captain was writing about Yolanda when I hit him."

"What, that note Detective Churchill showed me?"

"That note that said you were the best. He was going to write a review about you and your yummery, but then I hit him, knocked him right out! Bam! Right on the side of the head with my purse. That night I was so mad I wanted to kill him."

"I'm sorry to hear that," Yolanda said.

"No, you're not," Lydia snapped. "All you care about is your stupid yummery. Neither one of those Magical Cakes of Love worked. I know that the Valencia orange cake didn't. The chocolate one might have but these two dummies ate it before I had a chance to serve it to the captain. Yeah, and get this, they were staring like morons at some dumb movie on the TV when I walked in. I don't know what's so magical about that."

"It was really good," Richie said, and then stared at Teagan's tank top. "I wish you'd take that off and show us a good time," he moved closer to the bed, but Lydia kicked him.

"Have some common sense. You can't behave like that." Lydia said. "Maybe after we split the money you can but not till then."

"Yeah, Lydia, you were really loving it when we were walking around Yolanda's neighborhood last weekend," Richie said.

Yolanda stared at them. "You mean you…"

Lydia grinned. "I had him dress up like the captain and I dressed like you, so we pretended like the captain, and you were, you know, dating. Of course, it was done at night…and I bet your neighbors noticed…"

"That explains those sightings," Yolanda said. "It just didn't make any sense when Detective Churchill said it."

"See how smart I am?" Lydia laughed loudly, and pulled back the hammer and cocked the gun.

CHAPTER 11

FRIDAY

Abby and Frederick Carter went to the yummery to check on their daughter before the store opened. "Dear, this is so unlike her not to answer," Abby said as she again pressed the speed dial. She left yet another message and the couple entered, aware of the fact that no one was in the eerily quiet shop. They looked around anyway, going into the unfinished Beverage Bar, and the break room and rest rooms. There was no sign of their daughter.

"Guess we go to her house and check that out. At least we can feed the cats if she's not there." Frederick said. "And try calling Teagan again."

"I will. Yolanda's got to be there. Where else could she be? I know she's coming in later but still, she's not ... oh I just hope she's safe." Abby pocketed her cell phone and the parents returned to their car.

* * *

Fridays were hectic at the yummery and on that sunny morning, the parents were running the place along with BB and

Nick. Jeannie arrived just before the store opened and at ten minutes past seven, Tank and Chopper showed up.

There was a conference in Yolanda's office as Abby and Frederick, worried as they were, didn't want the employees to know that Yolanda and Teagan were missing. Abby wanted to call the police, but Frederick kept reminding her that their daughter was a suspect. Although now she was a missing suspect and that was beyond worrisome.

"Look, I need to know where our daughter is," Abby told the men. "She's our only child, she's our life. If something unthinkable ever happened to her then we couldn't live with ourselves."

"We found out where Lydia lives. I gave Yolanda the address last night and told her to wait for us to investigate it," Tank said.

"You what? Why didn't you investigate it when you got it?" Frederick asked.

"We gotta make sure. This isn't a *Rambo* movie where you run in with guns blazing. You gotta be sure. You gotta have the cops on your side," Tank said. Pulling out his phone, he punched in a speed dial number. "I need to talk to Detective Churchill now. What? I don't care, interrupt him, this is a matter of life and death." He shook his head. "No, I'm not exaggerating, you idiot. What? You heard me. Gimme his voice mail then." He sighed and waited for several seconds. "Churchill? Here's our suspect Lydia Sloan's address. Harper-Palms Building. 866 Harper Lane, number 26." He clicked off his phone and repocketed it. "What a bunch of..." He headed for the door. "Let's roll, Chopper."

"Wait, what about us?" Frederick opened the office door and was about to step into the kitchen.

"Mr. Carter, do you know the first thing about what..."

Frederick rushed into the kitchen and saw a rolling pin on

the stainless-steel table. "Here's my weapon. Now let's roll, buddy."

Abby chuckled. "Dear, are you losing your mind? That's not a weapon."

Tank and Chopper were in the kitchen and BB walked in to check on the oven, and stepped back, startled at the sight of so many people in there.

The burly men led the way out of the yummery and the parking lot still showed no signs of any marked or unmarked police car. Nor were there any news vans. "Okay, looks like we go to Lydia's place," Tank said as he unlocked his Buick.

Minutes later, the big blue car pulled up to the red zone in front of the Harper-Palms Building. "Sir, you're blocking a fire hydrant," Abby pointed out.

"Like I care? I'll get the ticket fixed," Tank said as he headed out.

"Ticket? You better hope that your car doesn't get towed," Frederick said. "Not that I ever had it happen to me."

They raced up the wide stone steps to the main entrance, which was covered with a tall black wrought iron gate. Chopper approached the gate and grabbed the handle, jiggling it a few times. "I'll take care of this." He removed his billfold, flipping through it and finding a white card. Chopper took it out and ran it through the key code swiper a few times. The gate swung open, and he went through, returning his card to his wallet and put it back in his pocket. "Better than American Express," he said as they all headed for the staircase.

Upstairs they found the unit at the back of the building. Three men and one woman stood outside the apartment, concealed only by the potted palm tree. Chopper leaned forward, ear almost touching the door. He shook his head. "I'm not hearing anything. We go in, Tank?"

"Yep, we go in." He tested the door handle to make sure it

wasn't open. It was locked. "Back up everyone." Tank positioned himself so he was facing the door spreading his big feet on the concrete, bending his knees slightly, then turning his massive upper body forty-five degrees to his left and with lightning speed his right leg kicked up, the bottom of his shoe hit the door. With a loud thud, it crashed open. He ran inside, closely followed by his friend and Yolanda's parents.

The four of them ran through the apartment, finding no sign of anyone in the place. In the smaller bedroom, they noticed the bed with the messy covers and a spool of rope on the floor next to a pair of filthy socks and some empty fast-food bags.

"This doesn't look good," Abby said as she turned around and followed her husband back into the kitchen.

On the dining room table sat an open laptop. Tank sat down in front of it, staring at the web browsing history. "Got it!" he said, pointing at the screen. "Angeles National Forest." He looked around and saw a portable printer on top of a bookcase in the living room. The green light was on. "Wow is she ever dumb," he said, as he printed out the map of their last places they visited online.

Frederick went over and looked at the screen. "Yeah, but at five-sixteen they were looking at the 405 to the 5 down to Mexico." He scrolled and looked at another set of entries. "No, wait, an accident down in Irvine will probably take care of that route. Plus, Yolanda doesn't carry her passport with her."

"Lydia has an SUV. She can hide her in the back," Tank said.

"Let's stop talking and start moving," Abby said.

Tank smiled. "The lady's right." He waved the printed-out directions in his hand. "We'll follow this route...and hope they've taken it."

They ran out of the apartment and downstairs. When they

got to the car, they all jumped inside and buckled up. "Tank, how long will it take?" asked Abby.

"According to the directions, almost an hour. With the Electra Lady? A lot less."

The car was blowing through stop signs and soon was heading west on Santa Monica Boulevard, with Tank anxiously watching his rearview mirror. After another sharp lane change and blowing through a yellow into red stoplight, he glanced at his watch. "Makin' time. Hey, anyone know anything 'bout a black Beemer, um, looks like an M3 convertible? Guessing it's maybe six, seven years old?"

Frederick turned around and had a look. "Yeah. That's Zac Field. He's Yolanda's ex-boyfriend."

Tank roared past a pickup truck. "Ex ... on good or bad terms?"

"He's still a friend," Abby reported.

Tank grinned. "That's good news. We can always use backup."

There were six people in a lush grove of oak trees in the Angeles National Forest. On a hot summer's day, it was the perfect vacation spot, but not for any of them. Yolanda sat on the ground, still wearing yesterday's attire of a now-sweaty yellow polo shirt and soiled jeans. Her feet were blistered inside slip-on sneakers. Teagan's arms and knees were scraped and bruised; her skimpy tank top and shorts weren't designed for uphill forestry hikes. Dirty, tired Captain Angus wore sneakers with no socks and a worn tracksuit. His bandana was sweat soaked, and he leaned against a tree, sound asleep or unconscious; no one knew.

Equally sweaty were the cousins, Richie and Damian, as

they plunged their shovels in the earth, flipping the clumps of dirt behind them. They dug three separate holes.

The last person standing was the gun-toting mastermind of the scheme to get Captain Prescott's fortune: Lydia Sloan. Her posture was straight, and she sported an olive-green safari outfit. A pocketed hunting vest worn over a lightweight shirt was paired with a flared skort. Forest green knee socks brought a flash of local color and didn't detract from the comfortable hiking boots. The ensemble was topped off by a beige Livingstone pith helmet. "Hurry up, men. The sooner you do this the sooner we get our money."

Damian glared at her and said nothing but shoveled a little faster. After all, he was packing his favorite .45 and if Lydia got too much out of hand, he was liable to bury her in one of the graves he was digging.

Lydia sneered down at her three captives, concentrating on Teagan as she waved the gun with tireless gusto. "You think you're so pretty, Teagan. I wasn't good looking I was just smart. Of course, I'm still smart – smarter than all five of you put together. But even though I'm smart it's worse than if I was as pretty as you because you're so stupid."

Teagan was struggling to release her bound hands, but she only tore at her wrists and her face got redder with the exertion.

Yolanda leaned over and whispered, "Don't react to her. It's wasting your time and energy."

"I know it, but she's so damn irritating," Teagan replied, looking down at the earth.

"Hey, you want me to dig a fourth grave?" Richie asked.

"Graves for everyone but us—good idea." Damian said.

"Just as long as we don't have to go back to prison," Richie said, leaning on his shovel. "That damn third strike law will put us behind bars for life."

Lydia smiled. "I know that. Now get back to work."

Resting against a tree was a large blue cooler. Lydia went over to it and pulled out a chilled bottle of imported water. It was dripping with condensation, and she applied it to her forehead and back of neck, enjoying the sensation of the bottle cooling off her sweaty skin. She twisted off the cap and took a gulp. Then she walked over and handed it to Richie. "Share it with Damian, those fools don't need to waste any of our water." Lydia returned to the cooler, put the lid down and sat on it, watching the men digging the graves.

There was a sudden rustling sound. Lydia turned and looked in the direction of the noise. It happened again. She stood up, clutching the gun in both hands as she walked towards it. The closer she got, the more nervous she became, and the gun was noticeably shaking.

"AAAAhhhhhhahhhhhahhh!!!" The shout was earsplitting...and surprising.

Lydia backed away, trying to hold the gun in her trembling hands.

A flash of pale wood in the air above her. Was it a tree branch? A hand clutched it, then it grew closer, and there was a wooden rolling pin held by Frederick Carter. He was about to hit her with it when behind him came his wife, panting heavily from the uphill climb. "Frederick, she has a gun!"

"I can see that!" he said.

Tank and Chopper rushed into the clearing, both holding their guns. The cousins had stopped digging when they heard the shouting. Damian yanked out his gun and Richie approached them, wielding his shovel.

Abby strained to go forward and rescue her daughter, but Frederick held onto her waist. "Don't go over there yet. That loon and her goons are armed and dangerous."

"Who do think you are, calling me a loon?" Lydia asked, pointing the gun at him. "I oughtta..." she pulled the trigger and the gun blasted. The recoil and noise made her drop it and she fell to the ground.

Frederick also collapsed to the ground and screamed. "My arm! My arm! My arm's gone."

More shrieks and shouts. Yolanda and Teagan desperately strained against their ropes. The captain woke up and yelled: "Abandon ship! Throw over the lifeboats!"

Zac appeared brandishing his bright orange putter. "Where's Yolanda? What's going on here?" He looked at Frederick Carter lying on the ground, his shirt showing some blood on the shoulder. "What happened to you, Mr. Carter?"

"That woman shot my arm off."

"No, sir. Your arm's still there." Zac turned and saw Yolanda and Teagan tied up and went over to untie them.

Chopper opened the cooler and pulled out water bottles for the captives. He went to check on the captain who'd fallen asleep again. Looking at his bloody bandana, he said, "this man needs medical attention promptly."

More noise from the trail was heard as Detective Churchill and four uniformed officers rushed into the area, all holding their guns and looking around at the hullabaloo. "Get on the ground now," the detective told Zac who was in the process of untying Yolanda's cords.

Captain Angus was untied, and he sat up, looking straight ahead. "Man overboard!"

Yolanda was hugging her mother. An EMT who'd just hiked up with a forest ranger was bandaging her father. A helicopter was circling overhead, looking for a place to land in an area with fewer trees. Teagan watched as Lydia was handcuffed and led away. Her pith helmet had fallen to the ground.

CHAPTER 12

____

JUNE 23

From seven in the morning until six that evening, the yummery and the brand-new Beverage Bar were super busy. Yolanda's parents were helping ring up sales in the yummery. The newest employees Yolanda and Nigel had hired, Crystal Irwin and Quinn Hendrickson, were professional baristas. Quinn also had bakery experience and if he worked out as well as Nigel said he would, he might be joining BB in the kitchen. Even with her cast of regulars, there were long lines. The news vans were a welcome sight and Vern Hess was given so many cups of coffee to sample that he had to rush into the yummery's restroom after his broadcast.

Both online and in the newspapers, Lydia Sloan had gone from being a meek and mild accountant to the Safari Stalker. This was attributed to her "outlandish" attire, according to the Other Patrick Stewart, one of the first reporters to arrive at the site of the melee in the Angeles National Forest. Yolanda also had Detective Winston Churchill to thank for the now infamous photo of Lydia Sloan handcuffed, clad in full safari regalia, including her pith helmet which sat on her head at a slightly jaunty angle. The good detective had seen it on the ground and deduced that the only individual who would wear such a thing was Lydia, so he returned it to the owner. The resulting photo of Lydia looking defiantly at the camera in her safari duds was lampooned nationally and internationally. The social media pictures and video footage about the Prescott kidnapping made the late-night talk shows.

Blogdate: 06-21.

Topic: Loony Lydia Sloan – The Safari Stalker

By Patrick Stewart [click to watch full report]

Readers,

I'm standing outside the Harper-Palms Apartment Building in the Brentwood/West L.A. area. It looks like any other building in this usually quiet neighborhood. But this is where the grandson of the Prescott Moving Pictures empire, Captain Angus Prescott, was held captive for 12 days. Here, in unit 26 on the northwest corner. And who was the madman who held the 58-year-old man hostage for almost two weeks? Well, it wasn't a man at all. It was an accountant, Lydia Sloan. A woman who only wanted to get her hands on the captain's fortune. A woman who kidnapped the good captain, along with Yolanda Carter, the owner of Yolanda's Yummery, and her best friend, co-worker/model/actress/dancer, Teagan Mishkin.

Ms. Lydia Sloan had plans to become Mrs. Lydia Prescott, and reap the rewards of his many financial interests including a memorabilia collection valued at upwards of ten million dollars, an expensive yacht, and a Beverly Hills estate. She used her feminine skills to lure the captain into marriage. How to do this? Ply him with Yolanda's Yummery's famous Magical Cakes of Love. Maybe it would have worked but her co-conspirators and cousins, Richie and Damian Sloan, intercepted the delicious cakes. The cousins are being charged with an equal number of felony counts: attempted murder, kidnapping, and grand larceny. The cousins consumed the Magical Cakes of Love that were meant for the Captain and Lydia, who may have otherwise ended up at the Chapel of Love in Las Vegas. This case will go down in the annals of local crime history as the ineptest kidnapping since the kidnapping of Frank Sinatra, Jr.

The Sloan family failed miserably. None of them saw any money from their attempts to sell the captain's vast movie and sports memorabilia collection. Maybe this story should tell us to keep our belongings to a minimum. If you have anything worth selling put it on eBay as fast as you can.

Oh, and ladies, be careful about wearing safari clothing. Not everyone looks good in a skort, knee socks and a pith helmet.

By three o'clock, there was a slight lull and that was when Jeannie noted the time to Yolanda. "Looks like we won't be seeing that Lydia again. Not that anyone here misses her business."

"Not after what happened," Yolanda said.

The door opened and an elegantly dressed man walked in and admired the scenery. He grinned upon seeing Yolanda. "Hello sir, would you like to sample our brownies or our strawberry vanilla cookies?"

The man glanced at the sample tray that she was heading towards and at the display cases that were full enough to show off the tantalizing array of the yummery's brightly colored sweets. To celebrate that week's strawberry vanilla theme, all the decadent chocolate Magical Cakes of Love had one large fresh strawberry placed on top of them. "I'd like one of each," the man said, accepting a strawberry vanilla cookie that made him do a little jig. "I've read about how great this place is and I read right!"

As the yummery filled up with more appreciated guests, the man peeled off a thick roll of cash to pay for all his items. Nick helped the man carry the boxes and bags out to his white Lexus sedan and returned holding a twenty-dollar bill that he deposited in the jar.

TIPS – GIVE A LITTLE, GET A LOT!

"Very true," Nick said to Yolanda.

"You're right about that."

The store was busy until closing time, and a few minutes before six, Clarabelle and her mother arrived to buy cookies.

"I'm really glad they caught the Safari Stalker," Clarabelle said as she approached the counter.

"So is everyone around here," Yolanda said.

"Do you have any of those yummy stacks of oatmeal raisin cookies left?" Clarabelle asked.

Yolanda smiled, noticing the girl was looking at the shelves behind her and not seeing any stacks of cookies. Good thing she'd saved a package and hid it in the drawer with the girl's name on it. "I saved one just for you."

The girl sighed with relief as she saw Yolanda pull out a yellow package from a cabinet. "Oh good. It's for the big Hunter/Jumper event at the Calabasas Equestrian Center tonight. I'm in a new division!"

"That's wonderful. Congratulations! Here, it's a little gift for you and your horse. Hope you win!"

Abby and Frederick were hovering in the doorway waiting to lock up for the night. The adolescent in the sky-blue shirt and tan pants with high black boots was given a hug by Abby and a handshake by Frederick along with their best wishes for a successful event. The girl's face was flushed with embarrassment mixed with eagerness.

The door was closed and locked; the overhead lights were switched off. Yolanda and her parents were alone in the yummery, as everyone else had gone next door to the Beverage Bar.

"Darling, I think you need to go next door for a minute," her mother said.

She looked at the outlines of her parents in the window behind them. It was an overcast evening but there was still enough light to see in the store.

Yolanda walked to the back of the shop and made a left hand turn past the area that once contained the refrigerated beverage unit but now had two tables and chairs. She went into the Beverage Bar.

When she arrived, the lights were switched on and she saw a large sparkly HAPPY BIRTHDAY, YOLANDA banner hanging on the back wall. Yells and cheers were heard, and she saw all the employees, including Teagan who had just changed into a sultry black dress and rhinestone studded stilettos.

The bar was covered with a pink and white tablecloth. At the center of it was a three-tier birthday cake in the bakery's colors topped with a small yellow pith helmet. Yolanda burst out laughing when she saw it. "Thanks BB, I know that had to be you!"

BB went over to her boss and gave her a big hug. "I just hoped you'd like it. And the cake's chocolate."

"You can't ever go wrong with chocolate," Yolanda said.

There were colorful piles of presents and several balloons hanging on the tables and a bunch was handed to her by Zac. She accepted them, but her smile wasn't quite as bright.

"Happy birthday, Yo," he said. "Look, I've told you before

how sorry I was about the pillow talk with Lydia and the keys and…"

She grinned through bared teeth. "Not the time or place to discuss this, Zac."

"Yeah, well, I thought … Um me and Teagan helped plan this surprise party," Zac said, backing away slowly.

"Thank you," she said, looking around the room, seeing her friends and acquaintances, people she'd known for a long time and those she'd recently met. The construction workers, Gil Resnick, Pepe Menendez, and Lance Norton were there, as was Nigel Garvey, who was lately acting a lot friendlier towards her. Guests included the Other Patrick Stewart, Mike O'Neill, Detective Churchill, and her lawyer, Kyle Newman.

Captain Angus Prescott looked dapper in a clean white yacht hat, all new clothing from the expensive navy jacket to the white trousers with creases. He wore custom-made leather loafers that were gleaming with polish. He was clean-shaven and his eyes glowed as walked inside and stood next to Teagan, putting his arm around her. Yolanda smiled upon seeing the happy couple and went over to welcome them.

A few feet away, Lance pulled back a section of tablecloth and pointed out the countertop to BB, who was admiring it. "Yeah, so like it's real wood, um it's oak, not laminate," he said.

"That's what I thought," BB smiled. "It sure looks fine."

"Yeah, I've worked with reclaimed wood too and it's so cool. But I'm gonna be fulltime surfing real soon, dude. Then I can train for next year's US Open of Surfing in Huntington Beach."

Kyle Newman went over to the birthday girl and shook her hand. "I want to wish you a very happy birthday, Yolanda," he stared at her intently. "And I can say I was right, as usual."

"Thank you Kyle. You were right about…?"

"You. I knew all along that you were innocent." He leaned a

little closer and pushed back a stray lock of hair. "And you know that now I can date you because…" His cell phone made a loud beeping noise, and he jumped a little. He pulled it out of his shirt pocket and glanced at it. "I'll be back in a few…" he dashed off to the back of the shop.

Yolanda smiled and was about to walk over to the Beverage Bar when Nigel approached her and handed her a pale blue linen envelope. The elegant font made her name look old fashioned. "Thanks, Nigel," she said, opening it. She saw the pretty birthday card with a picture of a bright pink birthday cake and when she flipped the card open, a ticket fell out. He reached down before her to retrieve it and handed it to her.

"See, my love for skating's returned. I'm inviting you to the Jubilee Skating Showcase at the Skate Palace rink. I'm doing a pairs number with Emily Townsend, my cousin. I wanted it to be a surprise, but…" He cleared his throat. "Well, I'm dedicating the number we're skating exclusively to you. I wanted you to know that I'm not cheating on you, sweetsie." He reached over and kissed her tenderly on the lips. "It's you and only you." Nigel reluctantly pulled away and smiled at her.

Out of the corner of her eye, she saw flowers looming ever closer. It was an abundant array of pink carnations and red roses, along with pink tulips and green, fuchsia and blue hydrangeas. The floral display was presented in a white basket. Holding the huge arrangement was Mike O'Neill. He winked at her. "Here you go, miss, I wanted you to know how much I admire and respect you…I hope you got my other flower arrangements?"

She accepted the beautiful blooms and smiled, edging over to the table to set the heavy gift down. "Thank you so much, Mike, yes I did."

"Good," he sidled up to her and put his arm around her. "I'd never want to rush a gal like you. I think you're marriage material!" He gave her a gentle kiss on the cheek and blew in her ear. She shivered and then he didn't wait for her to respond as he walked away. Suddenly she saw Detective Churchill barely manage to avoid bumping into Mike.

"Excuse me," the detective said, addressing the back of the blue jean and checkered shirt-wearing Texan. The detective faced Yolanda and gave her a winsome smile, making him appear younger than her. "I put my gift on the table," the detective said, pointing to a medium sized red box with a matching bow on the top. "Hey, when are you going to carry doughnuts in the yummery? I know the men at the station would be happy to come over and buy them right up!"

"Honestly, it's not going to happen this year. We've got our fall lineup of new products, but so far it's not doughnuts. And it's not one of my specialties. But who knows, if enough people ask for them then I might hire an expert doughnut maker."

"I'll be sending everyone in my department over. Well, I still recommend the yummery anyway," he said, and reached over and patted her hand. "You've been such a good sport about all this. I want you to know that. And I think the gift might … never mind, I think you got some company." The detective walked away.

The Other Patrick Stewart sauntered over and smiled apologetically at her. "Happy Birthday, Yolanda. I wish I could film this but Louie, my camera guy, couldn't make it." He reached over and gave her a hug. She hugged him back.

"That's okay. I'm just glad you showed up." She was being approached by two more guests.

Heather and Barry Hathaway had their arms around each other, and Heather looked adoringly at her husband. Yolanda noticed that he wore a soft green polo shirt that was tucked into a new pair of khaki shorts.

"Hey, Barry you look great," Yolanda exclaimed as she noticed his flat midsection emphasized by the form-fitting shirt.

"Thanks! I joined a gym and run for an hour every morning. Makes a world of difference!" He beamed and patted his stomach. "But I still eat a lot!"

"Barry has a good metabolism," Heather commented and gave him a peck on the cheek. "I have a special surprise for your birthday!" Heather looked in the direction of the table. "The big lavender box with the white ribbon..." she hugged her friend. "Open it later, though."

Yolanda nodded. "You've got me curious..."

Barry went back over to Yolanda and gave her a bear hug. "I want you to have a wonderful birthday, nothing but the best for you. Especially after what you went through with that crazy Safari Stalker."

"Thanks, Barry." He pulled away from her and went back over to his wife. "Where's Rosemary?"

Heather giggled. "She's scouting for a new wedding location. She looked at the farmer's almanac and saw that it'll be sunny on her big day so now it must be held outside! And she thinks it should be near the ocean."

Yolanda laughed. "Oh no!"

Heather and Barry nodded in unison. "We say that a lot when it comes to my sister. I hope that Gus, her fiancé, doesn't get cold feet. I wouldn't blame him if he does," Heather said.

Yolanda's parents stood next to the large birthday cake. Abby had just put the pink, yellow and green candles on the top layer of the cake, surrounding the yellow pith helmet. "Okay everyone," Frederick began and cleared his throat to get the partiers' attention. The talking stopped and those in attendance looked at Yolanda's parents standing next to the cake. "Just wanted to wish Yolanda a very happy twenty-eighth birthday!"

"Oh Dad, you promised you wouldn't tell!" Yolanda blushed.

There was a lot of laughter, especially from her parents. "It's okay, dear, next year we won't say a thing. You're still under thirty and you'll always be our baby."

Yolanda's face was on fire with her mother's pronouncement. "Okay, okay, thanks. Now can we cut the cake?" Yolanda went over to the cake, grabbed the pith helmet off the top and held it just over her head. "Thanks BB, I'm gonna save this!" She put it down and watched as her mother lit the candles.

The End

Valencia Orange Cupcakes
Recipe

I've made chocolate cupcakes with orange frosting before, but never a vanilla-based cupcake infused with freshly-squeezed orange juice. The batch turned out well and I even substituted olive oil for sunflower or safflower oil to see if there was a taste difference. Yes, it was a bit stronger and it wasn't as light and fluffy as it would've been if the usual vegetable oil had been used. I avoided using flavor oil but I added gel-based orange colorant for the cupcakes and frosting.

Cupcake ingredients:
    2 eggs, room temperature
    3/4 cup sugar
    1 1/4 cups cake flour
    1/2 cup vegetable oil
    1/2 cup orange juice
    1 teaspoon baking powder
    1 teaspoon vanilla extract
    1/4 teaspoon salt
    1 teaspoon orange flavor oil [optional]
    Orange colorant [optional]
    Oven temperature: 350 degrees Fahrenheit / 180 degrees Celsius
    Makes 9 cupcakes.
    Baking time: approximately 20 minutes

Directions: Preheat oven to 350 degrees Fahrenheit.

In a large mixing bowl, using a hand or stand mixer, beat the eggs and sugar until dissolved.

Add the oil and salt and mix for about a minute.

Add orange juice, flour and baking powder and mix until combined.

Add vanilla extract, flavoring and coloring.

Fill cupcake liners 3/4 full with batter.

Bake until a toothpick inserted into a cupcake comes out clean.

Cool cupcakes on a wire rack for a few minutes, and then remove cupcakes from pan and place on a wire rack to cool completely.

Orange Buttercream Frosting ingredients:
    6 ounces butter, softened
    1 1/4 Cup powdered sugar, sifted
    1 Tablespoon orange juice
    1 Tablespoon heavy cream
    1 Tablespoon orange zest for topping
    Orange flavor [optional]
    Orange colorant [optional]

Directions:

Beat softened butter on medium speed for about 2 minutes until smooth and creamy. Add powdered sugar, orange juice, cream, flavor, and colorant. Mix on high speed until well combined and smooth. Spoon into a piping bag with your favorite tip and pipe onto cooled cupcakes.

Chocolate Energy Bars Recipe

This one ticks a lot of boxes if you're looking for nut-free, vegan, low-sugar and an easy no-bake snack or dessert. It took me four tries to get it right. I'd also recommend storing them in the refrigerator, especially in warm weather.

Ingredients:

6 Tablespoons virgin coconut oil
5 Tablespoons organic coconut sugar
2/3 cup agave nectar
2 Tablespoons cocoa powder, sifted
1 1/2 cups crispy rice cereal
3 cups rolled oats
2 Tablespoons chia seeds
1/2 teaspoon Himalayan pink salt
1/2 cup chocolate chips

Instructions:

In a large glass measuring cup or bowl, combine the first four ingredients and stir well over medium heat. Remember to sift the cocoa powder before adding it to the oils and sugar so the mixture is smooth.

In a very large bowl, combine the rice cereal, rolled oats, salt, and chia seeds with a whisk.

Pour in the warmed up wet ingredients and mix well. Wait about 10 minutes to add the chocolate chips as you don't want them to melt completely.

In a parchment-lined 8" x 8" or 9" x 9" square pan, spoon in the mixture. Use a spatula to even out the top. Cover with plastic wrap and let sit on the counter for a few hours before slicing and eating.

If you're in a hurry, put it in the refrigerator for 2 hours.

Lastly, use a pizza cutter or sharp knife to cut the energy bars into squares or rectangles.

Store in the refrigerator. Wrap with waxed paper or plastic wrap.

Some substitutes:

If you want a buttery flavored energy bar, use butter instead of coconut oil.

Don't have any agave in your cupboard? No problem, use either honey or pure maple syrup.

About the Author

Lisa Maliga is an American author of contemporary fiction and cozy mysteries. Her nonfiction titles consist of how to make bath and body products with an emphasis on melt and pour soap crafting. When researching her fourth cozy mystery, she discovered the art of baking French macarons. She has written three dessert cookbooks, including two on macarons. When not writing, Lisa reads an assortment of books, takes photos, skates, and is working on a series of baking and soaping books and video tutorials.

You'll find more about her work at:

http://www.lisamaliga.com
http://lisamaliga.wordpress.com/
https://www.youtube.com/@LisaMaligaCreates
http://pinterest.com/lisamaliga/
https://truthsocial.com/@lisamaliga
http://www.goodreads.com/LisaMaliga
Newsletter http://eepurl.com/UZbE9

AUTHOR'S NOTE:

Thank you for taking the time to read *The Missing Sea Captain (A Yolanda's Yummery Cozy Mystery Series, Book 2)*. Feel free to write a review on any of the online bookstores. Also, please tell your friends, family, and friendly librarian about this book, along with any of my other titles!

FICTION:

Diary of a Hollywood Nobody - Chris Yarborough is a Midwesterner as green as the corn back home in Ohio. This former bookstore employee moves out to Los Angeles to pursue a profitable career in screenwriting.

Hollywood After Dark: 3 Tales of Terror – This trio of horror novelettes takes place in Los Angeles and Hollywood. Titles include *Satan's Casting Call*, *An Author's Nightmare*, and *Hollywood Starz Storage*. [Paperback and eBook]

I Almost Married a Narcissist - Charlotte White falls in love with a younger Romanian gymnastics coach. Andrei Antonescu is a sexy and handsome foreigner who loves to have fun and flirt with the ladies. The more she gets to know him, the more red flags are unfurled. Once she's able to see past his good looks and muscular body, Charlotte is unprepared for some shocking revelations.

I WANT YOU: Seduction Emails from a Narcissist - Arlen J. Stevenson is a narcissist who uses his scant literary accomplishments to entice his online victims. Meeting and seducing vulnerable women is what drives this Alabama-born man. [Paperback and eBook]

Love Me, Need Me: A Narcissist's Tale is about a bumbling sexual predator, narcissist, and author of three insipid zombie books. Middle-aged Arlen J. Stevenson hails from Alabama. His relentless and often hilarious pursuit of women online leads him to our other protagonist, Los Angeles-based writer of term papers, Helena Hoffman. [Paperback and eBook]

The Narcissist Chronicles: The WHOLE Story - Combined are the two narcissist novels: LOVE ME, NEED ME: A NARCISSIST'S TALE and I WANT YOU: SEDUCTION E-MAILS FROM A NARCISSIST.

North of Sunset - It's 1996 and Hollywood is thriving in the era of indulgences. Sherman Lee is a volatile and successful action movie producer who seeks critical acceptance. Ever the partier, his excesses are starting to take their toll. He can't keep a personal assistant more than a few days until Emily Karelin is sent to fill the position. She's a temp with no showbiz background, one of the requirements Sherman demands. [Paperback and eBook]

Notes from Nadir - A California writer returns to her Midwestern home due to financial difficulties. Moving in with Mom, she lands a job at an online auction site. She deals with wacky coworkers, unsympathetic relatives, health issues and the struggle with being in Nadir--the place and the state of mind. [Paperback and eBook]

Out of the Blue - Sylvia Gardner is a naïve cashier who lives with her mother in Richport, Illinois. Upset with being dumped by her first boyfriend; she later falls in love with an English actor after watching him on a TV show. For two years, she researches Alexander Thorpe's life and career, saving her money to travel to his Cotswolds village, intent on meeting him. [Paperback and eBook]

Satan's Casting Call - Duncan Smith-Holmes is a struggling young actor who is in desperate need of a paying gig or he has to leave Hollywood.

September Harvest - In this slice-of-life story set in September 1979, we meet Laurie Caswell a bookstore clerk at the Northbrook Mall. That Saturday night she goes to the movies with her boyfriend, Dennis Wayne. Later, they go to her house and share some booze. After he leaves, she has a vivid dream of the dying mall in 2021 and is shocked at the darkness that engulfs the future. Is it a dream, a nightmare, a vision, or a prophecy?

South of Sunset - Such a world-renowned name conjures up images of movies, sunglass-wearing stars, palm trees, plastic surgery, drug habits, the proverbial overnight success ... and the happy ending. In this collection of original short fiction, the author takes us into the minds of an assortment of losers, dreamers, successes, wannabes, and has-beens.

Sweet Dreams - Brenda Nevins is a successful romance author with a movie deal, a reality TV show, and a forthcoming bakery. Complications arise whenever any communication she sends or receives turns into fragments of a fantasy story. Will she find whoever is responsible for hijacking her career, finances, and even her fiancé?

NONFICTION:

12 Easy Melt and Pour Soap Recipes - Contains original recipes, 37 color photos, and several places to buy soap base, molds, fragrances and other necessary supplies. Learn how easy it is to craft your own melt and pour soap in less than one hour!

Baking French Macarons: A Beginner's Guide - Bake beautiful and delicious French macarons in your own kitchen. This collection of tried-and-tested recipes allows bakers to create these tasty and colorful confections.

Baking Chocolate Cupcakes and Brownies: A Beginner's Guide - It's easier than ever to bake decadent chocolate cupcakes and brownies. Get helpful tips about decorating and coloring cupcakes, recommended equipment, and loads of resources.

Baking Macarons: The Swiss Meringue Method - With

a photo of each recipe, this book offers everything you need to bake beautiful and delicious macarons. It features 20+ new tried-and-tested macaron recipes.

Dessert Cookbook Series: A Beginner's Guide - Includes 3 full-length dessert cookbooks and more than 55 recipes. Learn how to make many different desserts, no matter what your level of baking experience.

Fun Foodie Soap Crafting - You'll receive more than a dozen original and tested recipes, pretty packaging and labeling tips, 40+ photos, mistakes to avoid, and numerous supplier resources.

How to Make Handmade Shampoo Bars – Learn how easy it is to make natural handmade shampoo bars. This innovative eBook includes 25+ recipes for shampoo bars, hair rinses, and hair masques. Contains more than 50 color photos, step-by-step instructions, and a chapter on natural additives.

How to Make Handmade Shampoo Bars: The Budget Edition [Paperback only] – Same as above only with black and white photos.

Is the Long Island Medium the Real Deal? [Editor] - In this groundbreaking new book, author and demonologist Kirby Robinson examines Theresa Caputo's claims of mediumship and what's on The Other Side. [Paperback and eBook]

The Joy of Melt and Pour Soap Crafting is written by someone who learned how to work with crafting glycerin melt & pour soap the hard way -- with only a single page of instructions to follow! If you've always wanted to make your own soap, here's an opportunity to learn just how easy it really is! Contains 40 recipes and MUCH more!

Maple Sugar Melt & Pour Soap Recipe FREE at Smashwords. Learn how to make a fun fall melt and pour soap recipe starring pure maple syrup—a healthy addition.

Matcha Green Tea Melt & Pour Soap Recipe – Learn

how easy it is to make this luxurious melt and pour soap starring Matcha Green Tea. This soap is wonderful for all skin types. It would make a great addition to any bath and body or tea lover's gift basket! FREE at Amazon.

Monoi de Tahiti: Spa in a Bottle - What is Monoi de Tahiti and how will it benefit you? A bottle of this Polynesian beauty product has a variety of uses and will soothe your skin, hair, and nails. "Monoi de Tahiti: Spa in a Bottle" is a unique e-book focused on this fragrant and natural Tahitian beauty oil.

MORE Joy of Melt and Pour Soap Crafting - Two eBooks in one! You get *The Joy of Melt and Pour Soap Crafting* and *12 Easy Melt and Pour Soap Recipes* in one volume!

Nature's Beauty Oils: Monoi de Tahiti and Shea Butter – Two eBooks in one! Learn about nature's most versatile beauty oil and butter.

Never Mock God: An Unauthorized Investigation into Paranormal State's "I Am Six" Case - *Paranormal State*'s "I Am Six" episode is a perfect American horror tale -- for all the wrong reasons. It stars the ambitious founder of the Paranormal Research Society, an attention-seeking client, a bumbling group of paranormal investigators, a psychic-medium in search of ratings, and a rogue exorcist. [Paperback and eBook]

Nuts About Shea Butter - The reader will discover shea butter's benefits, its numerous applications, and how to get optimal use from this healthy and natural nut fat. Learn about the differences between East African and West African shea butter.

Organic and Sulfate Free Melt and Pour Glycerin Soap Crafting Recipes - If you want to make the most natural soap without using lye, here is a way to craft organic and sulfate free melt and pour glycerin soap at home. In less than an hour, you can craft lovely organic, sulfate free and eco-friendly Castile soaps with these carefully tested recipes.

Paranormal State Exposed [Co-Author] - Explore the rumors of staged scenes, questionable evidence, misleading editing, and duped clients. As other paranormal programming comes along imitating this style of presentation, it's vital that the problems are investigated.

Paranormal State: The Comprehensive Investigation [Co-Author] - Includes the eBooks *Paranormal State Exposed* and *Never Mock God: An Unauthorized Investigation into Paranormal State's "I Am Six" Case*.

The Prepper's Guide to Soap Crafting and Soap Storage - Be the cleanest prepper around! Create your own lye-free soap or find the best type of soap to store in the coming years. Informative book shows the best ways to craft your own soap. You'll receive original recipes and valuable storage tips to get the most out of your soap.

Rooibos Tea and Pink Kaolin Shampoo Bar Recipe - Discover how to craft rebatch/hand-milled soap base into a unique and versatile shampoo bar for most hair types. Also includes a recipe for Rooibos tea and apple cider vinegar hair rinse.

The Soapmaker's Guide to Online Marketing – This handy eBook is packed with detailed information on designing, building, and promoting your website. Learn how to write a press release. Get loads of free promotional ideas. Learn easy search engine optimization techniques and much more.

Squirrels in the Hood - When Sunshine the cat departs in 2006, the second story balcony she occupied is very empty. Now that birds can be fed, the author does so, also attracting an array of hungry squirrels.